No one belongs here more than you. Stories by Miranda July

SCRIBNER

New York   London   Toronto   Sydney

SCRIBNER
1230 Avenue of the Americas
New York, NY 10020

This book is a work of fiction. Names, characters, places,
and incidents either are products of the author's imagination or
are used fictitiously. Any resemblance to actual events or locales
or persons, living or dead, is entirely coincidental.

Copyright © 2007 by Miranda July

SCRIBNER and design are trademarks of
Macmillan Library Reference USA, Inc., used under license
by Simon & Schuster, the publisher of this work.

For information about special discounts for bulk purchases,
please contact Simon & Schuster Special Sales:
1-800-456-6798 or business@simonandschuster.com.

Text set in Bembo

Manufactured in the United States of America

5   7   9   10   8   6   4

Library of Congress Cataloging-in-Publication Data
July, Miranda, [date]
No one belongs here more than you: stories/by Miranda July.
p. cm.
Contents: The shared piano—The swim team—Majesty—The man
on the stairs—The sister—This person—It was romance—Something
that needs nothing—I kiss a door—The boy from Lam Kien—
Making love in 2003—Ten true things—The moves—Mon plaisir—
Birthmark—How to tell stories to children.
1. Short stories, American. I. Title.
PS3610.U537N6 2007
813'.6—dc22
2006051156

ISBN-13:   978-0-7432-9939-8
ISBN-10:   0-7432-9939-6

Page 205 constitutes an extension of the copyright page.

For Julia Bryan-Wilson

Contents

No one
belongs
here more
than you.

The Shared Patio

It still counts, even though it happened when he was unconscious. It counts doubly because the conscious mind often makes mistakes, falls for the wrong person. But down there in the well, where there is no light and only thousand-year-old water, a man has no reason to make mistakes. God says do it and you do it. Love her and it is so. He is my neighbor. He is of Korean descent. His name is Vincent Chang. He doesn't do hapkido. When you say the word "Korean," some people automatically think of Jackie Chan's South Korean hapkido instructor, Grandmaster Kim Jin Pal; I think of Vincent.

What is the most terrifying thing that has ever happened to you? Did it involve a car? Was it on a boat? Did an animal do it? If you answered yes to any of these questions, then I am not surprised. Cars crash, boats sink, and animals are just scary. Why not do yourself a favor and stay away from these things.

Vincent has a wife named Helena. She is Greek with blond hair. It's dyed. I was going to be polite and not mention that it was dyed, but I really don't think she cares if anyone knows. In fact, I think she is going for the dyed look, with the roots showing. What if she and I were close friends. What if I borrowed her clothes and she said, That looks better on you, you should keep it. What if she called me in tears, and I had to come over and soothe her in the kitchen, and Vincent tried to come into the kitchen and we said, Stay out, this is girl talk! I saw something like that happen on TV; these two women were talking about some stolen underwear and a man came in and they said, Stay out, this is girl talk! One reason Helena and I would never be close friends is that I am about half as tall as she. People tend to stick to their own size group because it's easier on the neck. Unless they are romantically involved, in which case the size difference is sexy. It means: I am willing to go the distance for you.

If you are sad, ask yourself why you are sad. Then pick up the phone and call someone and tell him or her the answer to the question. If you don't know anyone, call the operator and

*tell him or her. Most people don't know that the operator has
to listen, it is a law. Also, the postman is not allowed to go
inside your house, but you can talk to him on public property
for up to four minutes or until he wants to go, whichever
comes first.*

Vincent was on the shared patio. I'll tell you about this patio.
It is shared. If you look at it, you will think it is only Helena
and Vincent's patio, because their back door opens on to it.
But when I moved in, the landlord said that it was the patio
for both the upstairs and downstairs units. I'm upstairs. He
said, Don't be shy about using it, because you pay just as much
rent as they do. What I don't know for sure is if he told Vincent and Helena that it is a shared patio. I have tried to demon-
strate ownership by occasionally leaving something down
there, like my shoes, or one time I left an Easter flag. I also try
to spend exactly the same amount of time on the patio as they
do. That way I know we are each getting our value. Every time
I see them out there, I put a little mark on my calendar. The
next time the patio is empty, I go sit on it. Then I cross off
the mark. Sometimes I lag behind and have to sit out there a
lot toward the end of the month to catch up.

Vincent was on the shared patio. I'll tell you about Vincent. He is an example of a New Man. You might have read
the article about the New Men in *True* magazine last month.
New Men are more in touch with their feelings than even
women, and New Men cry. New Men want to have children, they long to give birth, so sometimes when they cry, it

is because they can't do this; there is just nowhere for a baby to come out. New Men just give and give and give. Vincent is like that. Once I saw him give Helena a massage on the shared patio. This is kind of ironic, because it is Vincent who needs the massage. He has a mild form of epilepsy. My landlord told me this when I moved in, as a safety precaution. New Men are often a little frail, and also Vincent's job is art director, and that is very New Man. He told me this one day when we were both leaving the building at the same time. He is the art director of a magazine called *Punt*. This is an unusual coincidence because I am the floor manager of a printer, and we sometimes print magazines. We don't print *Punt*, but we print a magazine with a similar name, *Positive*. It's actually more like a newsletter; it's for people who are HIV-positive.

Are you angry? Punch a pillow. Was it satisfying? Not hardly. These days people are too angry for punching. What you might try is stabbing. Take an old pillow and lay it on the front lawn. Stab it with a big pointy knife. Again and again and again. Stab hard enough for the point of the knife to go into the ground. Stab until the pillow is gone and you are just stabbing the earth again and again, as if you want to kill it for continuing to spin, as if you are getting revenge for having to live on this planet day after day, alone.

Vincent was on the shared patio. I was already behind in my patio use, so it made me a little anxious to see him there so late in the month. Then I had an idea; I could sit there with him. I put on Bermuda shorts and sunglasses and suntan oil. Even though it was October, I still felt summery; I had a summery tableau in mind. In truth, though, it was quite windy, and I had to run back for a sweater. A few minutes later, I ran back for pants. Finally, I sat in a lawn chair beside Vincent on the shared patio and watched the suntan oil soak through the fabric of my khakis. He said he always liked the smell of suntan oil. This was a very graceful way of acknowledging my situation. A man with grace, that's the New Man. I asked him how things were going at *Punt,* and he told me a funny story about a typo. Because we are in the same business, he didn't have to explain that "typo" is short for "typographical error." If Helena had come out, we would have had to stop using our industry lingo so that she could understand us, but she didn't come out because she was still at work. She's a physician's assistant, which may or may not be the same thing as a nurse.

I asked Vincent more questions, and his answers became longer and longer until they hit a kind of cruising altitude and I didn't have to ask, he just orated. It was unexpected, like suddenly finding oneself at work on a weekend. What was I doing here? Where was my Roman Holiday? My American in Paris? This was just more of the same, an American in America. Finally he paused and squinted up at the sky, and I guessed he was constructing the perfect question for me, a fantastic question that I would have to rise up to, drawing from everything I knew about myself and mythology and this black earth. But he was pausing only to emphasize what he was saying about how the cover design was not actually his fault, and then at last he did ask me something; he asked, Did *I* think it was his fault, you know, based on everything he had just told me? I looked at the sky just to see what it felt like. I pretended I was pausing before telling him about the secret feeling of joy I hide in my chest, waiting, waiting, waiting for someone to notice that I rise each morning, seemingly with nothing to live for, but I do rise, and it is only because of this secret joy, God's love, in my chest. I looked down from the sky and into his eyes and I said, It wasn't your fault. I excused him for the cover and for everything else. For not yet being a New Man. We fell into silence then; he did not ask me any more questions. I was still happy to sit there beside him, but that is only because I have very, very low expectations of most people, and he had now become Most People.

Then he lurched forward. With a sudden motion, he leaned forward at an inhuman angle and stayed there. It was not the behavior of Most People, nor of New Men; it was perhaps something that an old man would do, an elderly man. I said, Vincent. Vincent. I yelled, Vincent Chang! But he only leaned forward silently, his chest almost to his knees. I knelt down and looked into his eyes. They were open, but closed like a store that is closed and looking ghostly with all the lights off. With the lights off, I could now see how luminous he had been the moment before, even in his selfishness. And it struck me that maybe *True* magazine had been wrong. Maybe there are no New Men. Maybe there are only the living and the dead, and all those who are living deserve each other and are equal to each other. I pushed his shoulders back so that he was upright in his chair again. I didn't know anything about epilepsy, but I had imagined more shaking. I moved his hair out of his face. I put my hand under his nose and felt gentle, even breaths. I pressed my lips against his ear and whispered again, It's not your fault. Perhaps this was really the only thing I had ever wanted to say to anyone, and be told.

I pulled up my chair and leaned my head against his shoulder. And although I was genuinely scared about this epileptic seizure I was in charge of, I slept. Why did I do this dangerous and inappropriate thing? I'd like to think I didn't do it, that it was in fact done to me. I slept and dreamed that Vincent was slowly sliding his hands up my shirt as we kissed. I could tell my breasts were small from the way his palms were curved. Larger breasts would have required a less acute angle. He held them as if he had wanted to for a long time, and suddenly, I saw things as they really were. He loved me. He was a complex person with layers of percolating emotions, some of them spiritual, some tortured in a more secular way, and he burned for me. This complicated flame of being was mine. I held his hot face and asked him the hard question.

What about Helena?

It's okay, because she's in the medical profession. They have to do whatever is the best for health.

That's right, the Hippocratic oath.

She'll be sad, but she won't interfere with us because of the oath.

Will you move your things up to my apartment?

No, I have to keep living with Helena because of our vows.

Your vows? What about the oath?

It'll be okay. All that is nothing compared to our thing.

Did you ever really love her?

Not really, no.

But me?

Yes.

Even though I have no pizzazz?

What are you talking about, you perfect thing.

You can see that I'm perfect?

It's in each thing that you do. I watch you when you hang your bottom over the side of the bathtub to wash it before bed.

You can see me do this?

Every night.

It's just in case.

I know. But no one will ever enter you in your sleep.

How can you promise that?

Because I'm watching you.

I thought I would have to wait until I died for this.

From now on I am yours.

No matter what? Even when you are with Helena and I am just the short woman upstairs, am I still yours then?

Yes, it is a fact between us, even if we never speak of it again.

I can't believe this is really happening.

And then Helena was there, shaking us both. But Vincent kept sleeping, and I wondered if he was dead and, if so, had he said the things in the dream before or after he passed away, and which was more authentic. Also, was I a criminal? Would I be arrested for negligence? I looked up at Helena; she was a swarm of action in her physician's-assistant clothes. All the motion made me dizzy; I shut my eyes again and was about to reenter the dream when Helena yelled, When did the seizure start? And, Why the fuck were you sleeping? But she was checking his vital signs with professional flourish, and the next time she looked at me, I knew I would not have to answer these questions because I had somehow become her assistant, the physician's assistant's assistant. She told me to run into their apartment for a plastic bag that would be on top of the refrigerator. I ran inside gratefully and shut the door.

Their apartment was very quiet. I tiptoed across the kitchen and pressed my face against the freezer, breathing in the complex smells of their life. They had pictures of children on their refrigerator. They had friends, and these friends had given birth to more friends. I had never seen anything as intimate as the pictures of these children. I wanted to reach up and grab the plastic bag from the top of the refrigerator, but I also wanted to look at each child. One was named Trevor, and he was having a birthday party this Saturday. *Please come!* the invitation said. *We'll have a whale of a time!* and there was a picture of a whale. It was a real whale, a photograph of a real whale. I looked into its tiny wise eye and wondered where that eye was now. Was it alive and swimming, or had it died long ago, or was it dying now, right this second? When a whale dies, it falls down through the ocean slowly, over the course of a day. All the other fish see it fall, like a giant statue, like a building, but slowly, slowly. I focused my attention on the eye; I tried to reach down inside of it, toward the real whale, the dying whale, and I whispered, It's not your fault.

Helena slammed through the back door. She briefly pressed her breasts against my back as she reached over me to grab the bag, and then she ran back outside. I turned and watched her through the window. She was giving Vincent a shot. He was waking up. She was kissing Vincent, and he was rubbing his neck. I wondered what he remembered. She was sitting on his lap now, and she had her arms wrapped around his head. They did not look up when I walked past.

The interesting thing about *Positive* is that it never mentions HIV. If it weren't for the advertisements—Retrovir, Sustiva, Viramune—you would think it was a magazine about staying positive, as in upbeat. For this reason it is my favorite magazine. All the other ones build you up just to knock you down, but the editors at *Positive* understand that you have already been knocked down, again and again, and at this point you really don't need to fail a quiz called "Are You So Sexy or Just So-So?" *Positive* prints lists of ways to feel better, kind of like "Hints from Heloise." They seem easy to write, but that's the illusion of all good advice. Common sense and the truth should feel authorless, writ by time itself. It is actually hard to write something that will make a terminally ill person feel better. And *Positive* has rules, you can't just lift your guidance from the Bible or a book about Zen;

they want original material. So far none of my submissions has been accepted, but I think I'm getting closer.

Do you have doubts about life? Are you unsure if it is worth the trouble? Look at the sky: that is for you. Look at each person's face as you pass on the street: those faces are for you. And the street itself, and the ground under the street, and the ball of fire underneath the ground: all these things are for you. They are as much for you as they are for other people. Remember this when you wake up in the morning and think you have nothing. Stand up and face the east. Now praise the sky and praise the light within each person under the sky. It's okay to be unsure. But praise, praise, praise.

The Swim Team

This is the story I wouldn't tell you when I was your girl-friend. You kept asking and asking, and your guesses were so lurid and specific. Was I a kept woman? Was Belvedere like Nevada, where prostitution is legal? Was I naked for the entire year? The reality began to seem barren. And in time I realized that if the truth felt empty, then I probably would not be your girlfriend much longer.

I hadn't wanted to live in Belvedere, but I couldn't bear to ask my parents for money to move. Every morning I was shocked to remember I lived alone in this town that wasn't even a town, it was so small. It was just houses near a gas station, and then about a mile down, there was a store and that was it. I didn't have a car, I didn't have a phone, I was twenty-two, and I wrote my parents every week and told them stories about working for a program called R.E.A.D. We read to at-risk youth. It was a state-funded, pilot program. I never decided what the letters R.E.A.D. stood for, but every time I wrote "pilot program," I kind of marveled at my ability to come up with these phrases. "Early intervention" was another good one.

This story won't be very long, because the amazing thing about that year was that almost nothing happened. The citizens of Belvedere thought my name was Maria. I never said it was Maria, but somehow this got started, and I was overwhelmed by the task of telling all three people my real name. These three people were named Elizabeth, Kelda, and Jack Jack. I don't know why Jack twice, and I am not completely sure about the name Kelda, but that's what it sounded like, and that's the sound I made when I called her name. I knew these people because I gave them swimming lessons. This is the real meat of my story because of course there are no bodies of water near Belvedere and no pools. They were talking about this in the store one day, and Jack Jack, who must be dead by now because he was really old, said it didn't matter anyways because he and Kelda couldn't swim, so they'd be liable to drown themselves. Elizabeth was Kelda's cousin, I think. And

Kelda was Jack Jack's wife. They were all in their eighties, at least. Elizabeth said that she had swum many times one summer as a girl while visiting a cousin (obviously not cousin Kelda). The only reason I joined the conversation was that Elizabeth claimed you had to breathe underwater to swim.

That's not true, I yelled. These were the first words I'd spoken out loud in weeks. My heart was pounding like I was asking someone out on a date. You just hold your breath.

Elizabeth looked angry and then said she'd been kidding.

Kelda said she'd be too scared to hold her breath because she'd had an uncle who died from holding his breath too long in a Hold-Your-Breath contest.

Jack Jack asked if she actually believed this, and Kelda said, Yes, yes I do, and Jack Jack said, Your uncle died of a stroke, I don't know where you get these stories from, Kelda.

Then we all stood there for a little while in silence. I was really enjoying the companionship and hoped it would continue, which it did because Jack Jack said: So you've swum.

I told them about how I'd been on a swim team in high school, and even competed at the state level, but had been defeated early on by Bishop O'Dowd, a Catholic school. They seemed really, really interested in my story. I hadn't even thought of it as a story before this, but now I could see that it was actually a very exciting story, full of drama and chlorine and other things that Elizabeth and Kelda and Jack Jack didn't have firsthand knowledge of. It was Kelda who said she wished there was a pool in Belvedere, because they were obviously very lucky to have a swim coach living in town. I hadn't said I was a swim coach, but I knew what she meant. It was a shame.

Then a strange thing happened. I was looking down at my shoes on the brown linoleum floor and I was thinking about how I bet this floor hadn't been washed in a million years and I suddenly felt like I was going to die. But instead of dying, I said: I can teach you how to swim. And we don't need a pool.

We met twice a week in my apartment. When they arrived, I had three bowls of warm tap water lined up on the floor, and then a fourth bowl in front of those, the coach's bowl. I added salt to the water because it's supposed to be healthy to snort warm salt water, and I figured they would be snorting accidentally. I showed them how to put their noses and mouths in the water and how to take a breath to the side. Then we added the legs, and then the arms. I admitted these were not perfect conditions for learning to swim, but, I pointed out, this was how Olympic swimmers trained when there wasn't a pool nearby. Yes yes yes, this was a lie, but we needed it because we were four people lying on the kitchen floor, kicking it loudly as if angry, as if furious, as if disappointed and frustrated and not afraid to show it. The connection to swimming had to be enforced with strong words. It took Kelda several weeks to learn how to put her face in the water. That's okay, that's okay! I said. We'll start you out with a kickboard. I handed her a book. That's totally normal to resist the bowl, Kelda. It's the body telling you it doesn't want to die. It doesn't, she said.

I taught them all the strokes I knew. The butterfly was just incredible, like nothing you've ever seen. I thought the kitchen floor would give in and turn liquid and away they would go, with Jack Jack in the lead. He was precocious, to say the least. He actually moved across the floor, bowl of salt water and all. He'd come pounding back into the kitchen from a bedroom lap, covered with sweat and dust, and Kelda would look up at him, holding her book in both hands, and just beam. Swim to me, he'd say, but she was too scared, and it actually takes a huge amount of upper-body strength to swim on land.

I was the kind of coach who stands by the side of the pool instead of getting in, but I was busy every moment. If I can say this without being immodest, I was *instead* of the water. I kept everything going. I was talking constantly, like an aerobics instructor, and I blew the whistle in exact intervals, marking off the sides of the pool. They would spin around in unison and go the other way. When Elizabeth forgot to use her arms, I'd call out: Elizabeth! Your feet are up, but your head is going down! And she'd madly start stroking, quickly leveling out. With my meticulous, hands-on coaching method, all dives began with perfect form, poised on my desktop, and ended in a belly flop onto the bed. But that was just for safety. It was still diving, it was still letting go of mammalian pride and embracing gravity. Elizabeth added a rule that we all had to make a noise when we fell. This was a little creative for my taste, but I was open to innovation. I wanted to be the kind of teacher who learned from her students. Kelda would make the sound of a tree falling, if that tree were female. Elizabeth would make "spontaneous noises" that always sounded exactly the same, and Jack Jack would say, Bombs away! At the end of the lesson, we would all towel off and Jack Jack would shake my hand and either Kelda or

Elizabeth would leave me with a warm dish, like a casserole or spaghetti. This was the exchange, and it made it so that I didn't really have to get another job.

It was just two hours a week, but all the other hours were in support of those two. On Tuesday and Thursday mornings, I'd wake up and think: Swim Practice. On the other mornings, I'd wake up and think: No Swim Practice. When I saw one of my students around town, say at the gas station or the store, I'd say something like: Have you been practicing that needle-nose dive? And they would respond: I'm working on it, Coach!

I know it's hard for you to imagine me as someone called "Coach." I had a very different identity in Belvedere, that's why it was so difficult to talk about it with you. I never had a boyfriend there; I didn't make art, I wasn't artistic at all. I was kind of a jock. I was totally a jock—I was the coach of a swim team. If I had thought this would be at all interesting to you I would have told you earlier, and maybe we would still be going out. It's been three hours since I ran into you at the bookstore with the woman in the white coat. What a fabulous white coat. You are obviously completely happy and fulfilled already, even though we only broke up two weeks ago. I wasn't even totally sure we were broken up until I saw you with her. You seem incredibly faraway to me, like someone on the other side of a lake. A dot so small that it isn't male or female or young or old; it is just smiling. Who I miss now, tonight? is Elizabeth, Kelda, and Jack Jack. They are dead, of this I can be sure. What a tremendously sad feeling. I must be the saddest swim coach in all of history.

Majesty

I am not the kind of person who is interested in Britain's royal family. I've visited computer chat rooms full of this type of person, and they are people with small worlds, they don't consider the long term, they aren't concerned about the home front; they are too busy thinking about the royal family of another country. The royal clothes, the royal gossip, the royal sad times, especially the sad times, of this one family. I was only interested in the boy. The older one. At one time I didn't even know his name. If someone had shown me a picture, I might have guessed who he was, but not his name, not his weight or his hobbies or the names of the girls who attended that co-ed university of his. If there were a map of the solar system, but instead of stars it showed people and their degrees of separation, my star would be the one you had to travel the most light-years from to get to his. You would die getting to him. You could only hope that your grandchildren's children would get to him. But they wouldn't know what to do; they wouldn't know how to hold him. And he would be dead; he would be replaced by his great-grandson's beautiful strapping son. His sons will all be beautiful and strapping royalty, and my daughters will all be middle-aged women working for a local nonprofit and spearheading their neighborhood earthquake-preparedness groups. We come from long lines of people destined never to meet.

All my life I have had the same dream. It's what they call reoccurring; it always unfolds to the same conclusion. Except for on October 9, 2002. The dream began as it always does, in a low-ceilinged land where everyone is forced to crawl around on hands and knees. But this time I realized that everyone around me was having sex, it was a consequence of living horizontally. I was furious and tried to pry the couples apart with my hands, but they were stuck together like mating beetles. Then, suddenly, I saw him. Will. In the dream I recognized he was a celebrity, but I didn't know which one. I felt very embarrassed because I knew he was used to being around cute young girls and he had prob- ably never seen anyone who looked like me before. But gradually I realized he had lifted up the back of my skirt and was nuzzling his face between my buns. He was doing this because he loved me. It was a kind of loving I had never known was possible. And then I woke up. That's how I used to end all my stories in school: *And then I woke up!* But that wasn't the end, because as I opened my eyes, a car drove by outside and it was blaring music, which usually I hate and actually I think it should be illegal, but this song was so beautiful—it went like this: "All I need is a miracle, all I need is you." Which exactly matched the feeling I was having from the dream. I got out of bed and, as if I needed more evidence, I opened *The Sacramento Bee,* and there, in the World News section, was an article about Prince Charles's visit to a housing estate in Glasgow, a trip he took with his son, Prince William Arthur Philip Louis. There was a picture. He looked just as he had when nuzzling my buns, the same lovely blond confidence, the same nose.

I typed "royal family" into a dream-interpretation website, but they didn't have that in their database, so then I typed "butt" and hit "interpret," and this came back: *To see your buttocks in your dream represents your instincts and urges.* It also said: *To dream that your buttocks are misshapen suggests undeveloped or wounded aspects of your psyche.* But my butt was shaped all right, so that let me know my psyche was developed, and the first part told me to trust my instincts, to trust my butt, the butt that trusted him.

That day I carried the dream around like a full glass of water, moving gracefully so I would not lose any of it. I have a long skirt like the one he lifted, and I wore it with a new sexual feeling. I swayed in to work; I glided around the staff kitchen. My sister calls these skirts "dirndls." She means this in a derogatory way. In the afternoon she came by my office at QuakeKare to use the Xerox machine. She seemed almost surprised to see me there, as if we had bumped into each other at Kinko's. QuakeKare's mandate is to teach prepared-ness and support quake victims around the world. My sister likes to joke that she's practically a quake victim, because her house is such a mess.

What do you call that exactly, a dirndl? she said.

It's a skirt. You know it's a skirt.

But doesn't it seem strange that the well-tailored, flatter-ing piece of clothing that I'm wearing is also called a skirt? Shouldn't there be a distinction?

Not everyone thinks shorter is more arousing.

Arousing? Did you just say "arousing"? Were we talking about arousal? Oh my God, I can't believe you just said that word. Say it again.

What? Arousing.

Don't say it! It's too much, it's like you said "fuck" or something.

Well, I didn't.

No. Do you think you might never fuck again? When you said Carl left you, that was the first thing that came into my mind: She will never fuck again.

Why are you like this?

What? Should I be all buttoned up, like you? Hush-hush? Is that healthier?

I'm not that buttoned up.

Well, I would love to go out on that limb with you, but I'm going to need some evidence of this unbuttonedness.

I have a lover!

But I did not say this, I did not say I am loved, I am a person worth loving, I am not dirty anywhere, ask Prince William. That night I made a list of ways to meet him in reality:

Go to his school to give a lecture on earthquake
    safety.
Go to the bars near his school and wait for him.

They were not mutually exclusive; they were both reasonable ways to get to know someone. People meet in bars every day, and they often have sex with people they meet in bars. My sister does this all the time, or she did when she was in college. Afterward she would call and tell me every detail of her night, not because we are close—we are not. It is because there is something wrong with her. I would almost call what she does sexual abuse, but she's my younger sister, so there must be another word for it. She's over the top. That's all I can say about her. If the top is here, where I am, she's over it, hovering over me, naked.

The next morning I woke up at six and began walking. I knew I'd never be thin, but I decided to work toward an allover firmness that would feel okay if he touched me in the dark. After I lost ten pounds, I would be ready to join a gym; until then I would just walk and walk and walk. As I moved through the neighborhood, I re-ignited the dream, reaching such a pitch of clarity that I felt I might see him around the next corner. Upon seeing him, I would put my head under his shirt and stay there forever. I could see sunlight streaming through the stripes of his rugby pullover; my world was small and smelled like man. In this way I was blinded and did not see the woman until she stepped right in front of me. She was wearing a yellow bathrobe.

Shit. Did you see a little brown dog run that way? Potato! No.

Are you sure? Potato! He must have just run out. Potato! I wasn't paying attention.

Well, you would have seen him. Shit. Potato!

Sorry.

Jesus. Well, if you see him, grab him and bring him back over here. He's a little brown dog, his name is Potato. Potato!

Okay.

I walked on. It was time to concentrate on meeting him; plans 1 and 2. I've gone to other schools and discussed earthquake safety, so it wouldn't be the first time. There's a school in the neighborhood, Buckman Elementary, and every year they invite the firemen in to explain how to Stop, Drop, and Roll, and later in the day I come in and talk about earthquake safety. Sadly, there is very little you can do. You can stop, you can drop, you can jump up in the air and flap your arms, but if it's the Big One, you're better off just praying. Last year a little boy asked what made me the expert, and I was honest with him. I told him I was more afraid of earthquakes than any person I knew. You have to be honest with children. I described my reoccurring nightmare of being smothered in rubble. Do you know what "smothered" means? I acted out the word, gasping with my eyes popping out, crouching down on the carpet and clawing for air. As I recovered from the demonstration, he put his hand on my shoulder and gave me a leaf that was almost in the shape of a shark. He said it was the best one; he showed me other ones he had collected, all of them more leaf than shark. Mine was the sharkiest. I carried it home in my purse; I put it on the kitchen table; I looked at it before I went to bed. And then in the middle of the night, I got up and pushed it down the garbage disposal. I just don't have room in my life for such a thing. One question is: do they even have earthquakes in England? If they don't, this is the wrong approach. But if they don't, I have one more reason to want to live in the palace with him rather than convincing him to move into my apartment.

Then Potato ran by. He was a little brown dog, just like the woman said. He tore past me like he was about to miss a plane. He was gone by the time I even realized it had to be Potato. But he looked joyful, and I thought: Good for him. Live the dream, Potato.

Forget the school visit. I would step into the pub. That's what they call a bar over there. I would step into the pub. I would be wearing a skirt like the one he lifted in the dream. I would see him there with his friends and bodyguards. He wouldn't notice me, he would be shining, each golden hair on his arms would be shining. I would go to the jukebox and put on "All I Need Is a Miracle." This would give me confidence. I would sit at the bar and order a drink and I would begin to tell a yarn. A yarn is the kind of story that winds people in, like yarn around two hands. I would wind them in, the other people at the counter. There would be one part of the story that involved participation, something people would be compelled to chant at key moments. I haven't thought of the story yet, but I would say, for example: "And again I knocked on the door and yelled," and then everyone at the bar would chant: "Let me in! Let me in!" Eventually, all the people around me would be chanting this, and the circle of chanters would grow as they gathered in curiosity. Soon William would wonder what all the fuss was about. He would walk over with a bemused smile. What are the commoners doing now? I would see him there, so near to me, to every part of me, but I would not stop, I would keep spinning the yarn, and the next time I knocked on the door, he would shout with everyone else: Let me in! Let me in! And somehow this story, this amazing story that had already drafted half the English countryside, would have a punch line that called upon William alone. It would be a new kind of punch line, totally unlike "orange you glad I didn't say banana." This punch line would pull him to me, he would stand before me, and with tears in his eyes, he would beg me: Let me in! Let me in! And I would press his giant head against my chest, and because the yarn wasn't quite over I would say:

Ask my breasts, my forty-six-year-old breasts.

And he would yell into them, muffled: Let me in, let me in!

And my stomach, ask my stomach.

Let me in, let me in!

Get down on your knees, Your Highness, and ask my vagina, that ugly beast.

Let me in, let me in, let me in.

The sun was collapsing with a glare that seemed prehistoric; I felt not only blinded but lost, or as if I had lost something. And again she appeared, the woman in the yellow bathrobe. This time she was in a little red car. She had not even put on her clothes; she was still wearing the robe. And she was yelling "Potato" so desperately that she was forgetting to stick her head out the window, she was yelling into the interior of the car uselessly, as if Potato were within her, like God. Her vaulted cry was startling, a true wail. She had lost someone she loved, she feared for his safety, it was really happening, it was happening now. And I was involved, because amazingly, I had just seen Potato. I ran over to the car.

He just went that way.

What!

Down Effie Street.

Why didn't you stop him?

He was going so fast, it took me a moment to realize it was him.

It was Potato?

Yeah.

Was he injured?

No, he looked happy.

Happy? He was terrified.

As soon as she said this, I thought of how fast he was running and understood she was right. He was running in blind panic, in terror. A teenage Filipino boy walked up to the car and just stood there, the way people do when disaster strikes. We ignored him.

He went that way?

Yeah, but that was at least ten minutes ago.

Shit!

She roared off, down Effie Street. The boy stayed with me, as if we were together in this.

She lost her dog.

He nodded and glanced around, like the dog might be right nearby.

What's the reward?

I don't think there is one yet.

She has to have a reward.

This seemed crass to me, but before I could say so, the red car returned. She was driving slowly now. She rolled down her window, and I walked over with a spilled feeling inside. She was in a nightie. The yellow bathrobe had been formed into a little nest on the passenger seat, and in the nest was Potato, dead. I said I was terribly sorry. The woman responded with a look that told me I alone was responsible and she would share no words with a professional dog killer. I wondered how many other things had flown past me into death.

Perhaps many. Perhaps I was flying past them, like the grim reaper, signaling the end. This would explain so much.

She drove off, and the boy and I were alone again. I was only a few blocks from my house, but it was hard to walk away. I didn't know what I would think about when I began moving again. William. Who was William. It felt perverse, almost illegal to think about him now. And exhausting. Suddenly it seemed as if our relationship took mountains of strength to maintain. She was probably burying the dog in her yard right now. I looked at the boy; he was the opposite of a prince. He had nothing. When my sister was in college, she used to sometimes take these boys home. She would call me the next morning.

I could see it in his pants, it was like half hard, so I could already tell it was big.

Please stop now.

But when he took off his pants, I almost shit on myself, I was like, Please honey, get that thing up in me, and quick!

I see.

And then he took out this tiny piece of black rope or something and tied it around his cock, and I'm like, What's that for? And he just laughed in this nasty little-boy way. And I put on these tacky panties that I just got, they have a zipper in front that goes all the way around to the back? But he didn't really like those, I guess, because he just pulled them off and told me to do myself. Have you ever heard a guy say it like that? Do yourself?

No.

Of course you haven't. Anyways, I was rubbing and rubbing and I was super wet and he's all pushing it in my face and I'm going crazy for it and then, you're not going to believe this, he jizzes all over my face. Before I even get it in. Can you believe that?

Yes.

Well, yeah, I guess so. I guess he was really young and he probably'd never seen such white pussy before.

And then my sister paused to listen to the sound of my breath over the phone. She could hear that I was done, I had come. So she said goodbye and I said goodbye and we hung up. It is this way between us; it has always been this way. She has always taken care of me like this. If I could quietly kill her without anyone knowing, I would.

I looked at the boy; he was looking at me as if we had already agreed on something. Just by standing beside him for a minute too long, I had somehow propositioned him. I couldn't leave him without some kind of negotiation.

You could wash my car.

For how much?

Ten dollars?

For ten dollars I won't do anything.

Okay.

I opened my purse and gave him ten dollars and he walked down Effie Street toward certain death and I walked home. In the reoccurring dream, everything has already fallen down, and I'm underneath. I'm crawling, sometimes for days, under the rubble. And as I crawl, I realize that this one was the Big One. It was the earthquake that shook the whole world, and every single thing was destroyed. But this isn't the scary part. That part always comes right before I wake up. I am crawling, and then suddenly, I remember: the earthquake happened years ago. This pain, this dying, this is just normal. This is how life is. In fact, I realize, there never was an earthquake. Life is just this way, broken, and I am crazy to hope for something else.

The Man on the Stairs

It was a quiet sound, but it woke me up because it was a human sound. I held my breath and it happened again, then again: it was footsteps on the stairs. I tried to whisper, There's someone coming up the stairs, but my breath was cowering, I couldn't shape it. I squeezed Kevin's wrist in units, three pulses, then two, then three. I was trying to invent a language that could enter his sleep. But after a while I realized I wasn't even squeezing his wrist, I was just pulsing the air. That's how scared I was; I was squeezing air. And still the sound continued, the man coming up the stairs. He was walking in the slowest possible way. He seemed to have all the time in the world for this, my God, did he have time. I have never taken such care with anything. That is my problem with life, I rush through it, like I'm being chased. Even things whose whole point is slowness, like drinking relaxing tea. When I drink relaxing tea, I suck it down as if I'm in a contest for who can drink relaxing tea the quickest. Or if I'm in a hot tub with some other people and we're all looking up at the stars, I'll be the first to say, It's so beautiful here. The sooner you say, It's so beautiful here, the quicker you can say, Wow, I'm getting overheated.

The man on the stairs was taking so long, I forgot the danger for whole moments at a time and almost fell back asleep, only to be awakened by him shifting his weight. I was going to die and it was taking forever. I stopped trying to alert Kevin because I was worried he would make a sound upon waking, like he might say, What? Or, What, honey? The man on the stairs would hear this and know how vulnerable we were. He would know my boyfriend called me honey. He might even hear my boyfriend's slight annoyance, his exhaustion after last night's fight. We both fantasize about other people when we're having sex, but he likes to tell me who the other people are, and I don't. Why should I? It's my own private business. It's not my fault he gets off on having me know. He likes to report it the second he comes, like a cat presenting the gift of a dead bird. I never asked for it.

I didn't want the man on the stairs knowing these things about us. But he would know. The second he threw on the lights and pulled out his gun, or his knife, or his heavy rock, the second he held the gun to my head, or the knife at my heart, or the heavy rock over my chest, he would know. He would see it in my boyfriend's eyes: *You can have her, just let me live.* And in my eyes, he would see the words: *I never really knew true love.* Would he empathize with us? Does he know what it's like? Most people do. You always feel like you are the only one in the world, like everyone else is crazy for each other, but it's not true. Generally, people don't like each other very much. And that goes for friends, too. Sometimes I lie in bed trying to decide which of my friends I truly care about, and I always come to the same conclusion: none of them. I thought these were just my starter friends and the real ones would come along later. But no. These are my real friends. They are people with jobs in their fields of interest. My oldest friend, Marilyn, loves to sing and is head of enrollment at a prestigious music school. It's a good job, but not as good as just opening your mouth and singing. La. I always thought I would be friends with a professional singer. A jazz singer. A best friend who is a jazz singer and a reckless but safe driver. That is more what I pictured for myself. I also imagined friends who adored me. These friends think I'm a drag. I fantasize about starting over and eliminating the film of dragginess that hangs over me. I think I have a handle on it now; there are three main things that make me a drag:

I never return phone calls.

I am falsely modest.

I have a disproportionate amount of guilt about these two things, which makes me unpleasant to be around.

———

After we pulled out of the gas station, we drove to a restaurant that Kevin thought I might like. But I was still thinking about the boy with the squeegee, and I systematically did the opposite of everything that Kevin wanted. I didn't order dessert or wine, just a little salad, which I complained about. But he did not give up; he made jokes, ridiculous jokes, in the car on the way back to my apartment. I steeled myself against laughter; I would rather die than laugh. I didn't laugh, I did not laugh. But I died, I did die.

The Sister

Many times people have asked if I would like to meet their sister. Some women never marry and don't fuss much with their appearance, and the years don't tiptoe around them. These women, they have brothers, and the brothers of such women often know a man like me, an old man who is alone. Men alone often have one or two large things wrong with them, but these are things that the brothers think their sisters should be able to live with. An example of such a problem is: still being in love with one's deceased wife. This wasn't my problem; I had never been in love with anyone, dead or alive.

But this is an example of the type of problem that men like me have, sizable. We are often introduced to people's sisters. Sisters come in all ages; this took me a while to realize. I have no siblings, but I remember boys in school talking about their sisters, and so I always imagined sisters being of a certain age, school age. Did I want to meet their sister? At first I was taken aback to see such a tall, elderly sister. But of course everyone is old now, even the beautiful sisters of the boys I knew in school. It has been so long since I met a little girl. Men like me, men alone, we are the least likely people to be introduced to little girls. And I can tell you in one word why this is. Rape.

Almost all the purses in the world are made at the one place, Deagan Leather. Even if they have different tags on them, even if one of them says MADE IN SRI LANKA and the other one says MADE WITH PRIDE IN THE USA, they were both assembled in Richmond, California, at Deagan. When you finish your twentieth consecutive year at Deagan, they throw you a party with hula punch, and you automatically get free purses for the rest of your life. Victor Caesar-Sanchez and I are the only two people who've gotten the party so far. We play a game called What Good Thing Can You Make Out of Unlimited Purses. An example of a good thing is a leather house, or a leather airplane that actually flies. I didn't know the name of Victor's wife until she died last year: it was Caroline. I guess she wasn't Mexican like him; I had pictured her Mexican this whole time. And I did not know he had a sister until he asked, Do you want to meet my sister? Her name was Blanca Caesar-Sanchez.

Again I made that mistake of imagining her a teenager. A teenager in a white dress. New little breasts. I did want to meet her.

He arranged for Blanca and me to meet at an AIDS benefit party. Many of the people there were in their twenties and thirties, and I wondered if they were Blanca or the friends of Blanca. I went out of my way to be tolerant of them. There were also people in their forties, fifties, sixties, and seventies, and these people had a chance of being Blanca, too, or the parents of Blanca, or grandparents or even great-grandparents of Blanca, if Blanca was a child. There were a few children running around, sisters of brothers, who could be Blanca or Blanca's grandchild. The evening wore on. Many times I saw Victor and he told me that he had just seen his sister but lost her again. Then he said that he had in fact sent her over to my table not fifteen minutes ago to introduce herself, and had I not met her? I had not.

Well, what did you think of her?

I didn't meet her!

Oh, I thought you said you had.

No, I said I had not, I had not.

Well, that is a shame. I think she left. She told me she liked you.

What?

She said she wants to see you again.

But I never met her!

Watch it, that's my sister you're talking about.

———

41

I am six foot three. I weigh 180 pounds. I have gray hair that is receded. I am not fit, but I have a naturally fast metabolism, so I am skinny. Except for my stomach.

Blanca came in and out of my life over the next few weeks, but she never came in far enough for me to see her. I failed to meet her in so many different ways that I began to know her anyway. I knew the qualities of her particular absence. I dressed up for it. I wore a suit that I had never gotten the hang of in the seventies, but now it felt all right. It's an unusual suit because it's light beige, almost off-white. You don't see that color much in big amounts, suit and jacket both. It became my uniform for not meeting Blanca.

Was she at the Tiny Bubble Lounge last night?

She was! Did she introduce herself?

No.

I told her you sometimes go there. She's been stopping by regularly.

I'd like to meet her.

And she'd like to meet you.

Victor, she's gotta introduce herself. I see her in my dreams.

And what does she look like?

She's an angel.

That's Blanca, that's the one.

Is she blond?

No, she's dark-haired, like me.

A brunette.

Well, I don't know about that.

You just said she was.

Yeah, I just don't like to hear my sister talked about that way.

Brunette? That's nothing bad.

Yeah. But it's how you said it.

"Brunette" said by a man who has to use two hands to jerk off each night, that's what she did to me. I knew when she was near because I started breathing harder. The whole feeling in the room changed: her smell wrapped itself around my face, and I just knew she was there and I couldn't stop thinking she was a teenager. Even though it made no sense. The bar was full of smoke and men, but I could see her, behind someone, just out of view, in tight jeans and tennis shoes, chewing gum, with pierced ears and some kind of band holding her hair back. A ribbon or some kind of plastic band. And pierced ears. I said that already. Okay. That's what I saw. Some may say that such a girl is not ready for a relationship with a man, especially a man in his late sixties. But to that I say: We don't know anything. We don't know how to cure a cold or what dogs are thinking. We do terrible things, we make wars, we kill people out of greed. So who are we to say how to love. I wouldn't force her. I wouldn't have to. She would want me. We would be in love. What do you know. You don't know anything. Call me when you've cured AIDS, give me a ring then and I'll listen.

There were many times a day when I needed her. When I walked or took the bus to Deagan, when I was in motion, and when I was still. When I was inspecting purses and all of them were perfect, down to the last grommet. Day after day, no flaws, just a building tension, a growing fog that could be cut only by a backward strap or a missing buckle. Some people go on forever without flinching, without crying out. But I cried, Blanca! When the sun became unusually high and bright, or when it sank, especially when it sank far below the hills and I felt something similarly bright falling down inside of me, I called, Blanca. I called out to my own heart, as if she were within me like an egg. White like an egg and not quite ready; about to be, like an egg.

I had never thought much about Victor, but now he became this exciting person because he was Blanca's brother. Victor thought of me differently, too, more as a member of his family. As if Blanca and I were already a couple. He invited me over to a family-style dinner with Blanca and their parents. It was in an old people's home, and Mr. and Mrs. Caesar-Sanchez were the oldest people I've ever met who were still alive. The food they ate was all intravenous. When I asked Mrs. Caesar-Sanchez where her daughter was, she looked so incredibly confused that I let it go. There was a picture of her on the wall, not Blanca but her mother, as a girl. She had Blanca's look in her eyes: come hither, come yon. Victor talked to his parents as if they understood him, but I knew they didn't. He gave them each a purse, the popular SOHO-style shoulder tote in pebbled leather. It didn't seem like his parents would ever stand again, and shoulder totes really demand standing. Walking, living, needing, caring, toting. It seemed they were so far beyond these things, but I don't know, my parents died before I was old enough to give them anything. Victor and I ate the Chinese fried chicken that we had brought with us, and then we all watched a show where couples compete at remodeling their kitchens. Victor drove me home, and we did not speak in the car because what was there to say. For the eighthundredthmillionthtrillionth time, she hadn't shown up.

I had never been in love, I had been a peaceful man, but now I was caught in agitation. I accidentally hurt myself with my own body, as if I were two clumsy people fighting. I held on to some things too tightly, ripping pages as I turned them, and let go of other things too suddenly, plates, breaking them. Victor sat with me at lunch all week and tried to interest me in things that were not interesting. Finally, he invited me over to his apartment to have drinks with Blanca. I could tell this was it. I had wowed their parents with my comfortable silence. Some people are uncomfortable with silences. Not me. I've never cared much for call and response. Sometimes I will think of something to say and then I will ask myself: Is it worth it? And it just isn't. I wore the same thing I had worn all the other times I thought I was going to meet her, the all-beige, but this time I was more careful. I tucked my shirt into my boxers before I pulled up my pants, and when I pulled them up, they stroked the hairs on my legs. I was noticing everything, I was electric.

Blanca, of course, was late. Victor and I laughed about this, and I really laughed because now it was really funny in a way it had not been before. Goddamn that girl! She knew how to tease a guy. Victor and I toasted to Blanca and her lateness. I filled her cup and drank it for her, here's to my girl! My little girl!

At midnight Victor cleared his throat and said there was something he hadn't told me.

She's not coming?

No, she's coming.

Oh, good.

But I had a little plan for tonight, for you and Blanca.

What.

I have E.

What?

E.

What's E?

Ecstasy.

Oh.

Have you ever had it?

No, I'll just stick with my beer.

You're gonna like this.

I had a joint once and I didn't feel right for a whole year.

This isn't like that; it'll make you nice and loose with Blanca.

I don't think she wants me loose.

Trust me, she does. She'll have the third tab when she comes in.

Blanca likes this stuff?

Of course.

Is she like a . . . wild, out-of-control teenager?

You know she is.

God, I thought maybe she was, but I didn't want to ask.

Just put it under your tongue, like this.

Okay. Is she seventeen?

Yeah. Now let's just listen to the music and wait for it to kick in.

We sat on Victor's couch and listened to Johnny Cash or someone who sounds like that. A cowboy singer singing his cowboy song. I thought about Blanca and could feel her coming closer. I could almost hear her shoes on the street below, the sound of her running up the stairs, the door flying open. I imagined this again and again, hoping the door would fly open at the exact moment that I was imagining it flying open, and it would be a dream come true. The music, the cowboy, was a part of this. It made the air thicker, like I was thinking on the outside of my head. My thoughts were in the air, riding the song like a horse. I began to think of Victor as the cowboy. And for some reason I said this. Even though I don't like call and response, I called out.

Victor.

Yeah.

It's like you're the cowboy.

Yeah. What cowboy?

Singing the song, the cowboy song.

That's me, all right. You hear that sadness in my voice.

I do.

There's a lot of sadness in me.

I can hear it.

I think you've got a similar pain.

I do. I want to see her so bad, Victor. You have no idea.

I know.

Can you just show me a picture? Please.

You know I can't do that.

Why not?

Come onto the couch.

I sat beside Victor and I knew it was happening, the drugs. He held my hand and I rubbed his arm harder and harder and it felt okay. But then the rubbing was all of us, the whole length of our giant old selves. It was like a humping thing. I was thinking of eagles humping each other and then I remembered they don't hump, they lay eggs. I pushed him away.

What if Blanca walked in? You're her brother.

Let's just take our shirts off. The pants can stay on.

Are you gay?

I said the pants can stay on.

When do these drugs stop? If I drink water, do they stop sooner?

Just let this happen. It's okay. Just let it happen. There's no Blanca.

I didn't believe him for three hours. I sat in Victor's bedroom and he stayed on the couch and we waited for the drugs to stop and I waited for Blanca. When the drugs were over, I suddenly knew he was right. It was as if I had been on the drug for the last three months, and now I was back. I came out of the bedroom and sat on the couch.

I feel like she's been killed.

I'm sorry.

Do you even have a sister?

No.

Why did you take me to meet your parents?

I wanted them to meet you before they died.

Oh.

It felt like the air was multiplying, and I couldn't even think about what Victor said because I was so worried I wouldn't be able to keep up with the air. I tried to think of myself as a breathing machine. I told myself: You won't die from overbreathing, because you are a breathing machine, specially calibrated to adjust to the changing amounts of air in the room.

He said, Tell me about the girls.

What girls?

You like little girls.

No, teenagers.

Where do you meet them?

What? I don't do that, I just think about it.

That's good.

Yeah. I wouldn't do that.

Not even with Blanca?

Yeah, I guess with Blanca, but she's—that's different.

You don't like grown women?

Not so far, not yet.

Have you ever had sex with a woman?

Yeah.

What about a man?

No.

Victor brought his arms around me and I felt sick in my stomach and my cock felt sick, too. It felt feverish and painful and I rubbed it just to clear my head. Victor rubbed it, too, with tears on his cheeks and lips. I wanted to punch him, punch a hole right through him and then fill that hole with my body, and I was, I was doing that. He was sobbing now the way Blanca would sob, like a child. When I came, I came on the couch; I didn't want to come inside him because of what sperm can do. But he ate it off the couch and then he kissed me with a deep tongue, so whatever sperm can do, it was doing it to me. We slept. It was the sleep of one hundred years. And when we woke, it was still night, and Victor reached across me and turned on the lamp.

We were two old men. Everything seemed ordinary, even overly ordinary. There was a fly in the room and it buzzed around in a way that told us nothing amazing had ever happened in this place. I began to think about work, about the new hires in grommeting. I had to remember to tell them about the missing clamp on the heat sealer. I knew if I said something about this, if I said the word "grommeting," then everything would be as it had been, forever, amen.

We'll have to talk to the new hires tomorrow.

Yeah? Didn't Albie train them on Wednesday?

Yeah, but the ones in—

I was about to say "grommeting," the word "grommeting" was pulling up from the wet darkness under my throat; the G was coming forth with the grimace that makes the G sound. But in that instant the buzzing fly lurched toward my ear, and with animal reaction, fierce and unthinking, I swung at it and knocked over the lamp. It broke more than was fitting, crashing and shattering as if it were a lamp twelve times its size. In a final gesture, the bulb exploded in fireworks that fell quietly, extinguishing themselves. We said nothing, but the sudden return of darkness seemed to be a question, raised like eyebrows, waiting. Whatever I did next, whatever I said, would decide me. I didn't say "grommeting," but the G stayed in my throat, gathering voice.

I growled.

And Victor turned to me, right away, pressing his face against my neck. The new life came easily after this, a growl.

This Person

Someone is getting excited. Somebody somewhere is shaking with excitement because something tremendous is about to happen to this person. This person has dressed for the occasion. This person has hoped and dreamed and now it is really happening and this person can hardly believe it. But believing is not an issue here, the time for faith and fantasy is over, it is really really happening. It involves stepping forward and bowing. Possibly there is some kneeling, such as when one is knighted. One is almost never knighted. But this person may kneel and receive a tap on each shoulder with a sword. Or, more likely, this person will be in a car or a store or under a vinyl canopy when it happens. Or online or on the phone. It could be an e-mail re: your knighthood. Or a long, laughing, rambling phone message in which every person this person has ever known is talking on a speakerphone and they are all saying, You have passed the test, it was all just a test, we were only kidding, real life is so much better than that. This person is laughing out loud with relief and playing the message back to get the address of the place where every person this person has ever known is waiting to hug this person and bring her into the fold of life. It is really exciting, and it's not just a dream, it's real.

They are all waiting by a picnic table in a park this person has driven past many times before. There they are, it's everyone. There are balloons taped to the benches, and the girl this person used to stand next to at the bus stop is waving a streamer. Everyone is smiling. For a moment this person is almost creeped out by the scene, but it would be so like this person to become depressed on the happiest day ever, and so this person bucks up and joins the crowd.

Teachers of subjects that this person wasn't even good at are kissing this person and renouncing the very subjects they taught. Math teachers are saying that math was just a funny way of saying "I love you." But now they are simply saying it, I love you, and the chemistry and PE teachers are also saying it and this person can tell they really mean it. It's totally amazing. Certain jerks and idiots and assholes appear from time to time, and it is as if they have had plastic surgery, their faces are disfigured with love. The handsome assholes are

plain and kind, and the ugly jerks are sweet, and they are folding this person's sweater and putting it somewhere where it
won't get dirty. Best of all, every person this person has ever
loved is there. Even the ones who got away. They hold this
person's hand and tell this person how hard it was to pretend
to get mad and drive off and never come back. This person
almost can't believe it, it seemed so real, this person's heart
was broken and has healed and now this person hardly knows
what to think. This person is almost mad. But everyone
soothes this person. Everyone explains that it was absolutely
necessary to know how strong this person was. Oh, look,
there's the doctor who prescribed the medicine that made
this person temporarily blind. And the man who paid this
person two thousand dollars to have sex with him three times
when this person was very broke. Both of these men are in
attendance, they seem to know each other. They both have
little medals that they are pinning on this person; they are
badges of great honor and strength. The badges sparkle in the
sunlight, and everyone cheers.

This person suddenly feels the need to check her post
office box. It is an old habit, and even if everything is going
to be terrific from now on, this person still wants mail. This
person says she will be right back and everyone this person
has ever known says, Fine, take your time. This person gets in
her car and drives to the post office and opens the box and
there is nothing. Even though it is a Tuesday, which is
famously a good day for mail. This person is so disappointed,
this person gets back in the car and, having completely forgotten about the picnic, drives home and checks the voice

mail and there are no new messages, just the old one about "passing the test" and "life being better." There are no e-mails, either, probably because everyone is at the picnic. This person can't seem to go back to the picnic. This person realizes that staying home means blowing off everyone this person has ever known. But the desire to stay in is very strong. This person wants to run a bath and then read in bed.

In the bathtub this person pushes the bubbles around and listens to the sound of millions of them popping at once. It almost makes one smooth sound instead of many tiny sounds. This person's breasts barely jut out of the water. This person pushes the bubbles onto the breasts and makes weird shapes with the foam. By now everyone must have realized that this person is not coming back to the picnic. Everyone was wrong; this person is not who they thought this person was. This person plunges underwater and moves her hair around like a sea anemone. This person can stay underwater for an impressively long time but only in a bathtub. This person wonders if there will ever be an Olympic contest for holding your breath under bathwater. If there were such a contest, this person would surely win it. An Olympic medal might redeem this person in the eyes of everyone this person has ever known. But no such contest exists, so there will be no redeeming. This person mourns the fact that she has ruined her one chance to be loved by everyone; as this person climbs into bed, the weight of this tragedy seems to bear down upon this person's chest. And it is a comforting weight, almost human in heft. This person sighs. This person's eyes begin to close, this person sleeps.

It Was Romance

This is how we are different from other animals, she said. *But keep your eyes open so you can see the cloth.* We all had white cloth napkins over our faces, and the light glowed through them. It seemed brighter under there, as if the cloth actually filtered out the darkness that was in the rest of the room—the dark rays that come off things and people. The instructor walked around as she talked so that she was everywhere at once. Her face and permed hair were forgotten; there was just the voice and the white light, and these two things combined felt like the truth.

You will never be a part of the world. She was standing quite near.

Humans make their own worlds in the small area in front of their face. Now she was across the room.

Why do you think we are the only animal that kisses? She was near again.

Because the area in front of our faces is our most intimate zone. She drew a breath. *This is why humans are the only romantic animal!*

We were quiet and wondering under our napkins. How did she know this? What about dogs? Don't dogs feel everything we do times one hundred? But we couldn't see to form a chain of doubt between each other's eyes. And her voice had a vibrant certainty that made believing her feel liberating and obvious. Why pull your finger back when you can just let it be part of the hand? It *is* the hand! Of course! Fingers and hands are all one thing, these distinctions are like shackles. I see the light; it is coming through the napkin.

The tiny world in front of your face is an illusion, and romance itself is an illusion!

We gasped. But it was a delayed gasp, we were a slow group. Even the distribution of the napkins had been hard to organize. We had finally settled on take one and pass the rest down.

Romance isn't real, and neither is your world under the cloth. But because you are human, you can never lift the cloth. So you might as well learn how to be the most romantic woman you can be. This is what humans can do: romance. You may now remove the cloth.

We felt we might not be able to, because we were human, but it slid right off, and the auditorium seemed darker than before. I had hoped we would now be another type of animal, one that could be part of the world. But the cloth was just a metaphor, and we were forty women gathered on a Saturday morning to become more romantic. One woman still had the napkin on her head, possibly asleep.

We worked hard because we wanted results. We mirrored each other, and we breathed in no and breathed out yes. We wrapped our hands around our ankles and pretended they were someone else's, and then we tried to run and pretended that someone else was trying to run, someone we loved, was trying to run away. We held them by the ankles and we breathed in no and breathed out yes and released the ankles and ran, all around the auditorium, forty women. Then we came back to the circle and talked about pheromones and other kinds of mists.

Remember, you don't have to make the whole world romantic, or even the whole bedroom. Just the small space in front of your face. A very manageable territory, even the working women will agree. Because when he looks at you (or she—romance has no biases!), he has to look through the air in front of your face. Is that space polluted? Is it rosy? Is it misty? Think about these questions during the lunch break.

We ate our sandwiches and looked at each other through the air in front of our faces. It looked clear, but maybe it wasn't. We thought hard about this while we drank the provided soda. This could change everything.

I got up and stood alone in the hallway and pressed my face to the wall. It was wood-paneled and smelled like pee, as so many things do. Romance. My apartment. Romance. My Honda. Romance. My skin condition. Romance. My job.

I turned my head and pressed my other cheek against the wall.

The bell was calling us back together for the wrap-up session. Romance. My utter lack of friends who shared my interests. Romance. The Soul. Romance. Life on other planets. Romance. I stared down the hall. Someone was down there. It was Theresa whom I'd partnered with during breath-mirroring. We had synchronized our breaths and then syncopated them, and then we had talked about how that felt and which was more romantic. Syncopated was the right answer.

I walked down the hall and saw that Theresa was sitting on the floor next to a chair. This is always a bad sign. It's a slippery slope, and it's best to just sit in chairs, to eat when hungry, to sleep and rise and work. But we have all been there. Chairs are for people, and you're not sure if you are one. I knelt beside her. I rubbed her back, and then I stopped because I thought it might be too familiar, but that felt cold, so I patted her shoulder, which meant I was only touching her a third of the time. The other two thirds, my hand was either traveling toward her or away from her. The longer I patted, the harder it became; I was too aware of the intervals between the pats and couldn't find a natural rhythm. I felt like I was hitting a conga drum, and then as soon as I thought of this, I had to beat out a little cha-cha-cha, and Theresa began to cry. I stopped with the patting and hugged her, and she hugged me back. I had made everything just horrible enough to bring Theresa's sadness down to the next level, and I joined her there. It was a place of overflowing collaborative misery, and we cried together. We could smell each other's shampoo and the laundry detergents we had chosen, and I smelled that she didn't smoke but someone she loved did, and she could feel that I was large but not genetically, not permanently, just until I found my way again. The snaps on our jeans pressed into each other and our breasts exchanged their tired histories, tales of being over- and underutilized, floods and famines and never mind, just go. We wetted each other's blouses and pushed our crying ahead of us like a lantern, searching out new and forgotten sadnesses, ones that had died politely years ago but in fact had not died, and came to life with a little water. We had loved people we really shouldn't have loved and then married other people in order to forget our impossible loves, or we had once called out hello into the cauldron of the world and then run away before anyone could respond.

Always running and always wanting to go back but always being farther and farther away until, finally, it was just a scene in a movie where a girl says hello into the cauldron of the world and you are just a woman watching the movie with her husband on the couch and his legs are across your lap and you have to go to the bathroom. There were things of this general scale to cry about. But the biggest reason to cry was to drench the air in front of our faces. It was romance. Not the falling-in-love kind but the sharing of air between our shoulders and chests and thighs. There was so much air to share. Gradually, we slowed, then stopped, and after a long, still pause—goodbye—we broke apart. Then the euphoria came, warm winds from Hawaii, drying our tears and clearing the path back to the material world. It was joy to be there, beside the chair. We held each other's hands and laughed with feigned embarrassment that gradually took hold and became real.

Theresa wiped off her backside briskly, as if she had taken a fall. I pulled down the cuffs of my cardigan. We walked down the hall and entered the auditorium just in time to help stack the chairs. There was no system for stacking, so we accidentally made many substacks that were too heavy to lift and join together. The stacks of various heights stood alone. We gathered our purses and walked to our cars.

Something That Needs Nothing

In an ideal world, we would have been orphans. We felt like orphans and we felt deserving of the pity that orphans get, but embarrassingly enough, we had parents. I even had two. They would never let me go, so I didn't say goodbye; I packed a tiny bag and left a note. On the way to Pip's house, I cashed my graduation checks. Then I sat on her porch and pretended I was twelve or fifteen or even sixteen. At all these ages, I had dreamed of today; I had even imagined sitting here, waiting for Pip for the last time. She had the opposite problem: her mom *would* let her go. Her mom had gigantic swollen legs that were a symptom of something much worse, and she was heavily medicated with marijuana at all times.

We're going now, Mom.

Where?

To Portland.

Can you do one thing for me first? Can you bring that magazine over here?

We were anxious to begin our life as people who had no people. And it was easy to find an apartment because we had no standards; we were just amazed that it was *our* door, *our* rotting carpet, *our* cockroach infestation. We decorated with paper streamers and Chinese lanterns and we shared the ancient bed that came with the studio. This was tremendously thrilling for one of us. One of us had always been in love with the other. One of us lived in a perpetual state of longing. But we'd met when we were children and seemed destined to sleep like children, or like an old couple who had met before the sexual revolution and were too shy to learn the new way.

We were excited about getting jobs; we hardly went anywhere without filling out an application. But once we were hired—as furniture sanders—we could not believe this was really what people did all day. Everything we had thought of as The World was actually the result of someone's job. Each line on the sidewalk, each saltine. Everyone had rotting carpet and a door to pay for. Aghast, we quit. There had to be a more dignified way to live. We needed time to consider ourselves, to come up with a theory about who we were and set it to music.

With this goal in mind, Pip came up with a new plan. We went at it with determination; three weeks in a row we wrote and rewrote and resubmitted our ad to the local paper. Finally, the *Portland Weekly* accepted it; it no longer sounded like blatant prostitution, and yet, to the right reader, it could have meant nothing else. We were targeting wealthy women who loved women. Did such a thing exist? We would also accept a woman of average means who had saved up her money.

The ad ran for a month, and our voice mailbox overflowed with interest. Every day we parsed through the hundreds of men to find that one special lady who would pay our rent. She was slow to come. She perhaps did not even read this section of the free weekly. We became agitated. We knew this was the only way we could make money without compromising ourselves. Could we pay Mr. Hilderbrand, the landlord, in food stamps? We could not. Was he interested in this old camera that Pip's grandmother had loaned her? He was not. He wanted to be paid in the traditional way. Pip grimly began to troll through the messages for a gentle man. I watched her boyish face as she listened and realized that she was terrified. I thought of her small bottom that was so like a pastry and the warm world of complications between her legs. Let him be a withered man, I prayed. A man who really just wanted to see us jump around in our underwear. Suddenly, Pip grinned and wrote down a name. Leanne.

The bus dropped us off at the top of the gravel driveway that Leanne had described on the phone. We had told her our names were Astrid and Tallulah, and we hoped "Leanne" was a pseudonym, too. We wanted her to be wearing a smoking jacket or a boa. We hoped she was familiar with the work of Anaïs Nin. We hoped that she was not the way she sounded on the phone. Not poor, not old, not willing to pay for the company of anyone who would drive all the way out to Nehalem, population 210.

Pip and I walked down the gravel path toward a small brown house. There was bad food being cooked, we could smell it already. And now a woman stepped onto the porch, she was frowning. Her age was hard to determine from our vantage point, a point in our lives when we could not bring older bodies into focus. She was perhaps the age of my mother's older sister. And, like Aunt Lynn, she wore leggings, royal-blue leggings, and an oversized button-down shirt with some kind of appliqué on it. My mind ballooned with nervous fear. I looked at Pip and for a split second I felt as though she was nobody special in the larger scheme of my life. She was just some girl who had tied me to her leg to help her sink when she jumped off the bridge. Then I blinked and was in love with her again.

She waves and we wave. We wave until we are close enough to say hi and then we say hi. Now we are close enough to hug, but we don't. She says, Come in, and inside, it is dark, with no children. Of course there are no children. Pip asks for the money right away, which is something we decided on beforehand. It is terrible to have to ask for anything ever. We wish we were something that needed nothing, like paint. But even paint needs repainting. Leanne tells

us we are younger than she expected and to sit down. We sit on an old vinyl couch and she leaves the room. It is a terrible room, with magazines piled everywhere and furniture that could have come from a motel. We don't look at each other or anything that is reflective. I stare at my own knees.

For a long time we don't know where she is, and then, slowly, I can feel that she is standing right behind us. I realize this just before she pulls her fingernails through my hair. I didn't think she was the sexual type, but now I see that I don't know anything. It has begun, and every second we are closer to the end. I say to myself that long nails equal wealth; the idea of wealth always calms me down. I pretend I smell perfume. What if we all used expensive shampoo. What if we were kidding all the time and cared about nothing. My head relaxes, and I do the exercise where you imagine you are turning into honey. My mind slows down to a rate that would not be considered functional for any other job. I am alive only one out of every four seconds, I register only fifteen minutes out of the hour. I see she is standing before us in a slip and it is not really clean and I die. I see that Pip is taking off her shoes and I die. I see that I am squeezing a nipple and I die.

On the long ride home, neither of us said anything. We were kites flying in opposite directions attached to strings held by one hand. The money we had just made was also in that hand. Pip stopped to get a bag of chips on the way home, and now we had $1.99 less than our rent. It seemed obvious now that we should have charged more. Pip put the money in an envelope and wrote *Mr. Hilderbrand* on it. Then we stood there, apart, bruised and smelling like Leanne. We turned away from each other and set about tightening all the tiny ropes of our misery. I ran a bath. Just before I stepped in the tub, I heard the front door close and froze midstep; she was gone. Sometimes she did this. In the moments when other couples would fight or come together, she left me. With one foot in the bath, I stood waiting for her to return. I waited an unreasonably long time, long enough to realize that she wouldn't be back tonight. But what if I waited it out, what if I stood here naked until she returned? And then, just as she walked in the front door, I could finish the gesture, squatting in the then-cold water. I had done strange things like this before. I had hidden under cars for hours, waiting to be found; I had written the same word seven thousand times attempting to alchemize time. I studied my position in the bathtub. The foot in the water was already wrinkly. How would I feel when night fell? And when she came home, how long would it take her to look in the bathroom? Would she understand that time had stopped while she was gone? And even if she did realize that I had done this impossible feat for her, what then? She was never thankful or sympathetic. I washed quickly, with exaggerated motions that warded off paralysis.

I paced around our tiny room. It didn't even occur to me to go outside; I had no idea how to navigate the city without her. There was only one thing I couldn't do when she was with me, so after a while, I lay down on the couch and did this. I closed my eyes. In all the well-worn memories, we were between the ages of six and eight. We were under the covers on her mom's foldout sofa, or on the top bunk of my bunk bed, or in a tent in her backyard. Every location was potent in its own way. No matter where we were, it began when Pip whispered, Let's mate. She scooted on top of me; we clamped our arms around each other's backs. We rubbed ourselves against each other's small hip bones, trying to achieve friction. When we did it right, the feeling came on like a head rush of the whole body.

But just before I got there, I noticed a clicking noise in the air. It was distractingly present, quietly insistent. I looked up. Above my head, our five Chinese paper lanterns were slightly rocking of their own accord. As I reached toward them, I suddenly realized why, but I was too late to stop myself. I shook a lantern, and from the hole in the bottom, cockroaches came pouring out. They were crawling even as they fell. They were planning the conquest of wherever they landed even before they touched down. And when they hit the ground, they didn't die, they didn't even think of dying. They ran.

When Pip finally came home, we agreed that the Leanne job was not worth the money. But a few days later, we saw Nastassja Kinski in the movie *Paris, Texas.* She was wearing a long red sweater and working in a peep show. I thought it looked like a pretty easy job, as long as Harry Dean Stanton didn't show up, but Pip didn't agree.

No way. I'm not gonna do that.

I could do it without you.

This made her so angry that she did the dishes. We never did this unless we were trying to be grand and self-destructive. I stood in the doorway and tried to maintain my end of our silence while watching her scratch at calcified noodles. In truth, I had not yet learned how to hate anyone but my parents. I was actually just standing there in love. I was not even really standing; if she had walked away suddenly, I would have fallen.

I won't do it, never mind.

You sound disappointed.

I'm not.

It's okay; I know you want them to look at you.

Who?

Men.

No, I don't.

If you do that, then I can't be with you anymore.

This was, in a way, the most romantic thing she had ever said to me. It implied that we were living together not because we had grown up together and were the only people we knew, but because of something else. Because we both didn't want men to look at me. I told her I would never work in a peep show, and she stopped doing the dishes, which meant she was okay again. But I wasn't okay. In the last ten years, we had touched only three times.

1. When she was eleven, her uncle tried to molest her. When she told me about it, I cried and she hit me on the chin and I curled up in a ball for forty minutes until she uncurled me. I kept my eyes shut as she pulled my knees

away from my chest and I could feel her looking at my body and I knew that if I kept my eyes closed it would happen and it did. She slid her hand under my tights and felt around until she had located the thing she knew on herself. Then she shook her finger in a violent, animal way that quickly gave me the old rush. When it was over, she told me not to tell anyone and I didn't know if she meant this, with me, or about her uncle.

2. When we were fourteen we got drunk for the first time, and for about nine minutes, everything seemed possible and we kissed. This encounter seemed promisingly normal, and in the following days I waited for more kissing, perhaps even some kind of exchange of rings or lockets. But nothing was exchanged. We each kept our own things.

3. In our last year of high school, I momentarily had one other friend. She was an ordinary girl, her name was Tammy, she liked the Smiths. There was no way I could ever be in love with her because she was just as pathetic as me. Every day she told me everything she was thinking, and I guessed that this was what most girls did together. I wanted to talk about myself, too, badly, but it was hard to know where to begin. She was always so far ahead of me, in the minutiae of poems she had written in reference to dreams she had dreamed. So I just hung out, in a loose imitation of Pip. Pip did not think much of Tammy, but she was mildly intrigued by the normalcy of the friendship.

What do you guys do?

Nothing. Listen to tapes and stuff.

That's it?

Last weekend we made peanut-butter cookies.

Oh. That sounds fun.

Are you being sarcastic?

No, it does.

So she came along the next time I went over to Tammy's house. This made me a little nervous because Tammy had these parents who were always around. Traditionally, parents did not know what to make of Pip, who looked much more like a boy than a girl, and somehow made mothers feel flirtatious and fathers feel strangely threatened. But Tammy's parents were watching a movie and just waved absently behind their heads when we came in. As predicted, we listened to tapes. Pip asked if we were going to make peanut-butter cookies, but Tammy said she didn't have the right stuff. Then she threw herself down on the bed and asked us if we were girlfriends or what? An appalling emptiness filled the room. I stared out the window and repeated the word "window" in my head, I was ready to *window window window* indefinitely, but suddenly, Pip answered.

Yeah.

Cool. I have a gay cousin.

Tammy told us that her room was a safe space and we didn't have to pretend, and then she showed us a neon pink sticker that her cousin had sent her. It said FUCK YOUR GENDER. We all looked at the sticker in silence, absorbing its two meanings—at *least* two, probably even more. Tammy seemed to be waiting for something, as if Pip and I would obediently fall upon each other the moment we read the sticker's bold command. I knew we were a disappointment, meekly sitting on the bed. Pip must have felt this, too, because she abruptly threw her arm over my shoulder. This had never happened before, so understandably, I froze. And then very gradually recalibrated my body into a casual attitude. Pip just blinked when I sighed and flopped my hand on her thigh. Tammy watched all of this and even gave a slight nod of approval before shifting her attention back to the music. We listened to the Smiths, the Velvet Underground, and the Sugarcubes. Pip and I did not move from our position. After an hour and twenty minutes, my back ached and my numb blue hand felt unaffiliated with the rest of my body. I politely excused myself.

In the powdery warmth of the bathroom I felt euphoric. Being alone suddenly felt wild. I locked the door and made a series of involuntary, baroque gestures in the mirror. I waved maniacally at myself and contorted my face into hideous, unlovable expressions. I washed my hands as if they were children, cradling one and then the other. I was experiencing a paroxysm of selfhood. The scientific name for this spasm is the Last Hurrah. The feeling was quickly spent. I dried my hands on a tiny blue towel and walked back to the bedroom.

I knew it the moment before I saw it. I knew I would find them together on the bed like this, I knew I would be stunned, I knew they would spring apart and wipe their mouths. Pip would not look me in the eye. I would never talk to Tammy again. I knew we would all graduate from high school, I knew that Pip and I would live together as planned. And I knew she did not want me in that way. She never would. Other girls, any girl, but not me.

———

Now that we had paid the rent, we felt entitled to mention the cockroach situation to the landlord. He said he would send someone over but that we shouldn't get our hopes up.

Why not?

Well, it's not just your apartment; the whole building's infested.

Maybe you should have them do the whole building, then.

It wouldn't do any good; they'd just come over from other buildings.

It's the whole block?

It's the whole world.

I told him never mind then and got off the phone quickly, before he could hear Pip hammering. We were making some renovations; specifically, we were building a basement. Our apartment was tiny, but the ceilings were tall, and there was a tantalizing amount of unused space above our heads. Pip thought lofts were for hippies, so even though our studio was on the second floor, she had sketched out a design that would allow us to live on a low-ceilinged main floor, and then, when feeling morose, descend a ladder to the basement. We would leave the heavy things down there, like the refrigerator and bathtub, but everything else would come upstairs. We could both picture the basement perfectly in our heads. It had a damp, mineral smell. Warmth and seams of light seeped through the ceiling. Up there was home. Dinner waited for us up there.

One of the many great reasons for building a basement was our access to free wood. Pip had met a girl whose father owned Berryman's Lumber and Supply. Kate Berryman. She was a year younger than us and went to the private high school by Pip's grandma's house. I had never met her, but I felt glad that we were using her. We practiced a very loose, sporadic form of class warfare that sanctioned every kind of thievery. There was no person, no business, no library, hospital, or park that had not stolen from us, be it psychically or historically, and thus we were forever trying to regain what was ours. Kate probably thought she was on our side of the restitution when she struggled to pull large pieces of plywood out of the back of her parents' station wagon. She left them in the alley behind our building, honking three times as she drove away. At her signal, we strolled out of the building, pretending to take a walk, sometimes even stopping to buy a soda, before arbitrarily, on a whim, deciding to amble down the alley. We hauled it upstairs, feeling fairly certain we had hoodwinked everyone. We were always getting away with something, which implied that someone was always watching us, which meant we were not alone in this world.

Each morning Pip made a list of what we needed to do that day. At the top of the list was usually *go to bank*, where they had free coffee. The next items were often vague—*find out about food stamps, library card?*—but the list still gave me a cozy feeling. I liked to watch her write it, knowing that someone was steering the day. At night we discussed how we would decorate the basement, but during the day our progress was slow. Mostly, what we had was a lot of pieces of wood; they leaned against the walls and lay across the couch like untrained dogs.

We were trying to nail a post into the linoleum kitchen floor when Pip decided we needed a certain kind of bracket.

Are you sure?

Yeah. I'll call Kate and she'll bring it.

Isn't she in school?

It's okay.

Pip made the call and then went to take a shower. I continued hammering long nails through the post and into the floor. The post became secure. It was a satisfying feeling. It wouldn't withstand any kind of weight, but it stood on its own. It was almost as tall as me, and I could not help naming it. It looked like a Gwen.

The buzzer rang, and Pip ran damply to the door. It was Kate. I looked up at her from where I was sitting on the kitchen floor. She was wearing a school uniform. She was not holding the brackets. Maybe she had hidden them up her skirt.

Where are the brackets? I asked.

With panic in her eyes, Kate looked at Pip. Pip took her hand, turned to me, and said, We have to tell you something.

I suddenly felt chilled. My ears felt so cold that I had to press my hands against them. But I quickly realized this made me look as if I were covering them to avoid listening, like the monkey who hears no evil. So I rubbed my palms together and asked, Are your ears cold? Pip didn't respond, but Kate shook her head.

Okay, go ahead.

Kate and I are going to live together at her parents' house.

Why?

What do you mean?

Well, I'm sure Kate's dad doesn't want you living in his house after you stole all that stuff from him.

I'm going to work at Berryman's Lumber to pay him back. I might even make enough money to get a car.

I thought about this. I imagined Pip driving a car, a Model T, wearing goggles and a scarf that blew behind her in the wind.

Can I work at Berryman's Lumber, too?

Pip was suddenly angry. Come on!

What? I can't? Just say I can't if I can't.

You are purposely not getting it!

What?

She raised Kate's hand, clasped in her own, and shook it in the air.

Suddenly my ears were hot, they were boiling, and I had to fan my hands at either side of my head to cool them down. This was too much for Pip; she grabbed her backpack and marched out of the apartment with Kate following.

I could not let her leave the building. I ran down the hall and threw myself on her. She shook me off; I locked my arms around her knees. I was sobbing and wailing, but not like a cartoon of someone sobbing and wailing—this was really happening. If she left, I would become mute, like those children who have witnessed horrible atrocities. No one would understand me but those children. Pip was pry-ing my fingers off her shins. Kate knelt to help her, and I was repulsed by the touch of her pudding-like skin, I wanted to puncture it, I lunged at her chest. Pip took this moment to scuttle down the stairs, and somehow Kate was behind her. I was holding Kate's cardigan. I ran after them, watched them hurry into Kate's car. Before they pulled away, I shut my eyes and hurled myself onto the sidewalk. I lay there. This was my last hope—that Pip would take pity on me. I heard their car idling. I listened to the traffic and the sound of pedestrians walking carefully around me. I could almost hear Kate and Pip arguing in the car, Pip wanting to get out and help me, Kate urging them to leave. I pressed my cheek against the pavement in prayer. High heels clicked toward me and stopped; an elderly woman's voice asked if I was okay. I whispered that I was fine and silently begged her to move on. But the woman was persistent, so finally I opened my eyes to tell her to go. Kate's car was gone.

I pulled the phone into the bed and slept for three days. At intervals I would open my eyes long enough to remember and then I'd drop back into unconsciousness. In dreams I knew I was tunneling toward her—if I could only dig deep enough, I would find her. The tunnels narrowed as I crawled through them, until they became impossibly knotted strands of hair that I could only tear at.

On the afternoon of the third day, the phone rang. I pulled it up from the loamy depths of the bed. I wanted her to know, from the moment she heard my voice, that I was dying. I delivered a salutation so craven, so wretched, that it fell through language like pebbles. Hello.

It was Mr. Hilderbrand, the landlord. In some bizarre, alternative, science-fiction reality, the rent was due. It was just one month ago that we had lifted Leanne's dirty slip. I hung up the phone and looked around the room. My post was still standing in the kitchen, tactfully silent. A dangerously tall table-like structure wobbled in the middle of the room. It was the first square foot of the upstairs. I crawled underneath it and imagined Pip and Kate eating dinner with Mr. and Mrs. Berryman. It was the kind of scenario Pip had often described. We could not walk past a fancy house without her presuming its owners would want her to live with them if only they knew she was available. She saw herself as a charming street urchin, a pet for wealthy mothers. It was a scam. There was nothing in the world that was not a con, suddenly I understood this. Nothing really mattered, and nothing could be lost.

I went to the bathroom and threw handfuls of water on my face, and it was easy. In fact, I could do anything. I took off the jeans and T-shirt I had been sleeping in. Naked, I crouched on the floor and sliced the legs off my pants with a box cutter. I put them on and they were itty-bitty. Itty-bitty teeny-tiny. I sawed through the T-shirt, leaving IF YOU LOVE JAZZ on the floor. HONK barely covered my small breasts, but hey. Hey, I was leaving the apartment. I was walking down the hall, and there was a small basket of old apples in front of the neighbor's door with a sign that said, FOR MY NEIGHBORS PLEASE TAKE ONE. And hey, I was starving. I took

an apple and the door swung open. I had never really seen
this neighbor, but now I could see that she was a junkie. An
old junkie. And she was wearing a sweater that I knew she
had found in the hallway. It was Kate's cardigan. She told
me to take another one, and then she asked for a hug. I
hugged her hard with an apple in each hand. Last week I
would have been afraid to touch her, but now I knew that
I could do anything.

I had no money for the bus, so I walked. It was an incredible distance. A horse would get tired galloping there. When
birds flew there, it was called migration. But it wasn't difficult, it just took time. It was a new experience to walk across
the city in tiny shorts and a half-shirt that said HONK. People
honked without even seeing the shirt. I often felt that I
would be shot in the back with an arrow or gun, but this
didn't happen. The world wasn't safer than I had thought; on
the contrary, it was so dangerous that my practically naked
self fit right in, like a car crash, it happened every day.

The place I was walking to was in a strip mall, between a
pet store and a check-cashing place. I asked the man at the
counter if they were hiring, and he gave me a form to fill out
on a clipboard. When I handed it back, he stared at it without moving his eyes, which made me think maybe he couldn't
read. He said I could start tonight if I wanted to come back
at nine. I said, Great. He said his name was Allen, I said my
name was Gwen.

I hung out in the strip mall for three hours. The pet store
was closed, but I could see the rabbits through the window.
I pressed my fingers against the glass, and an ancient lop-ear

hopped toward me wearily. It looked at me with one eye and then the other. Its nose quivered, and for a moment I felt that it recognized me. It knew me from before, like an old teacher or a friend of my parents. The rabbit's eyes darted across my clothes and sniffed my wild, sad urgency and guessed that I was up to no good. Then I stood up, brushed off my knees, and walked into Mr. Peeps Adult Video Store and More.

The "and More" part was in the back. Allen left me there with a woman named Christy. She was sitting in a green plastic patio chair and wearing a pink OshKosh overall dress. Looking at the sturdy gold overall fasteners, I wondered if everything familiar was actually part of a secret sexual underworld. She showed me into the booth and began packing dildos and bottles and strings of beads into a sporty Adidas bag. Adidas. Her tools were laid out on an old flowery towel, and I knew that if I smelled the towel, it would smell like my grandmother. Gramma. Christy wrapped the towel around a small empty jelly jar.

What's that for?

Pee.

Even pee was in on this. She showed me the price list and the slot that money would come through. She raised her hand through the air as she described how the curtain would roll up. She cleaned a telephone receiver with Windex and paper towel and told me to never leave it sticky. Then, with hasty efficiency, she pulled her long, thin hair into a ponytail, swung the Adidas bag over her shoulder, and left.

The store felt very quiet, like a library. I sat on the green plastic chair and adjusted my shirt and shorts. The fluorescent lights droned with a timeless constancy. I looked up at them and imagined that they, not the stars, had hung over the long creation of civilization. They had droned over ice ages and Neanderthals, and now they droned over me. I stood up and walked into my booth. I didn't have anything to lay out on a towel; I didn't even have a towel. All I had was the key to the apartment. If I didn't make any money tonight, I would be walking all the way back there. At night. In this outfit. I was in a unique situation where I needed to give a Live Fantasy Show in order to protect my personal safety.

I practiced taking the phone off the hook. I did it five times, quicker and quicker, as if this were the skill I would be paid for. I thought about the words that I would have to say into it. I had never said any of these words except as swear words. I tried to think of them as seductive. I tried to say them seductively into the receiver, but they came out in a swallowed whisper. What if I couldn't say them? How awkward would that be? The man would ask for his money back, and I wouldn't get to take the bus. In a panic, I said all the dirty words I knew in one long curse: *Cock-sucking ball-licking bitch whore cunt pussy-licking asshole fucker.* I hung up the phone. At least I could say them.

I sat in the plastic chair for more than three hours. During this time, two different men came into the store. They both peeked at me over the racks of videos, but neither of them walked to the back. After the second man left, Allen yelled out from behind the counter.

That's the second one you've let go by!

What?

You've gotta be more aggressive! Can't just sit on your ass back there!

Got it!

Twenty minutes later, a man in a black sweatshirt came in. He peered over a rack of magazines at me, and I rose to my feet and walked toward him. His sweatshirt had a picture of a galaxy on it with an arrow pointing to a tiny dot and the words YOU ARE HERE. The man looked up at me and pretended to be surprised. I imagined him instinctively pulling off his hat in the presence of a lady, but he wasn't wearing a hat.

Are you interested in a live fantasy show, sir?

Yeah. Okay.

He followed me to the back of the store. We parted for a moment and reunited inside the booth with the curtained glass between us. I heard a Velcro wallet ripping open, twenty dollars fell lightly into the locked plastic box, and the curtain rose. He already had his penis out and the phone in one hand. I lifted the receiver. But as I had feared, I was mute. I stood paralyzed, as if on a rock over a cold lake. I was never good at jumping in, letting go of one element and embracing another. I could stand there all day, letting the other kids go in front of me forever. He was pumping it up and down and it was a strange sight, not something you see every day; in fact, I had never seen this before. He said something into the phone, but I didn't catch it. Despite how close we were, the reception was not very good.

Excuse me?

Can you take off your clothes?

Oh. Okay.

From the start, one is trained not to take off your clothes in front of complete strangers. Keeping one's clothes on is actually the number one rule for civilization. Even a duck or a bear looks civilized when clothed. I pulled down my jean shorts and lifted my shirt over my head. I stood there naked, like a bear or a duck. The man looked at me with grim concentration, my pale breasts, the puff of hair between my legs, back and forth between these poles. He checked occasionally to make sure I was looking at him. I diligently stared at his penis and hoped that this was enough, but after a few seconds, he asked me if I liked what I saw. Again I was on the rock, kids splashed below me yelling Jump! But I knew jumping was like dying, I would have to let go of everything. I considered what I had. She hadn't called, she wouldn't call, I was alone, and I was here—not even in some abstract sense, not here on earth or in the universe, but really *here,* standing naked before this man. I pushed my hand between my legs and said: Your big hard cock is making me so horny.

At five A.M. I was gliding through the night on a bus. The bus was just a formality, though—actually I was flying, in the air, and I was taller than most people, I was nine or twelve feet tall, and I could fly, I could jump over cars, I could say "cock" ravenously, gently, coyly, demandingly, I could fly. And I had $325 in my pocket. Standing with one foot in the bathtub until she returned wasn't just a way to stop time, it was also a ritual to bring her back. I would be Gwen until she came home.

I bought a lime-green negligee, a dildo that I devirginized myself with, and a chestnut-colored wig in a bobbed style

84

called Élan. I hated my job, but I liked that I could do it. I had once believed in a precious inner self, but now I didn't. I had thought that I was fragile, but I wasn't. It was like suddenly being good at sports. I didn't care about football, but it was pretty amazing to be in the NFL. I told long, involved stories that revolved around my own perpetually wet pussy, I spread open every part of my body, I told customers I missed them, and these customers became regulars, and these regulars became stalkers. I learned to stay inside until the moment before my bus came, and then dash past anyone who was lurking in the parking lot, waving and yelling, Come see me on Thursday!

And I missed her terribly.

One evening the bus was late and a customer followed me out to the curb. He stood beside me at the bus stop and I ignored him and then he started spitting. First he spit on the pavement, then more generally in the air. I felt tiny wet specks blow onto my face and I pressed my lips together and stepped backward. He, too, stepped back, and continued to fill the air with his scattershot. His harassment relied on a logic so foreign that I felt disoriented, I couldn't gauge whether it was terrifying or silly, and it was this feeling that told me to go back inside. I walked and then ran, slamming the door behind me. But Mr. Peeps was not exactly a safe haven, and I couldn't stay there forever. I asked Allen to go outside and see if the customer was still there. He was. Couldn't Allen tell him to leave? Allen felt he could not because a) he wasn't breaking the law, and b) he was a good customer. Allen thought I should call a friend or a cab to pick me up.

I had been waiting for this moment, and I marveled at how organically it had arisen. I usually imagined poisoning myself or getting hit by a car. Someone official, a cop or a nurse, would ask if there was anyone I wanted them to call. I would gasp her name. She works at Berryman's Lumber and Supply, I would say. This situation was not as dire, but it involved safety, and more important, it wasn't my idea to call her. I had been ordered, almost commanded, by a superior, Allen.

I called Berryman's Lumber quickly, almost distractedly, modeling myself after the kind of person who would have a question about replacement saw blades. But the moment the line began ringing, my senses dilated, winnowing out everything that was not the ring or the sound of my own heart.

Berryman's Lumber and Supply, how can I help you?

I'm trying to reach Pip Greeley?

Just a sec.

Just a sec. Just two months. Just a lifetime. Just a sec.

Hello?

It's me.

Oh. Hi.

This wouldn't do. This Oh. Hi. I couldn't be the person who elicited a response like this. I straightened my wig. I smiled into the air the way I smiled when customers unbuckled their belts, and I made my eyes laugh as if everything were some version of a good time. I began again.

Hey, I'm in a bind here and wonder if you could help me out?

Yeah? What?

I'm working at this place, Mr. Peeps? And there's this really creepy guy hanging around. Do you have a car?

She was silent for a moment. I could almost hear the name Mr. Peeps vibrating in her head. It described a man with eyes the size of clocks. She had devoted her whole life to avoiding Mr. Peeps, and now here I was, cavorting with him. I was either repulsive and foolish, or I was something else. Something surprising. I held my breath.

She said she guessed she could borrow a van, and could I wait twenty minutes until she got off work? I said I probably could.

We didn't talk in the van, and I didn't look at her, but I could feel her looking at me many times with bewilderment. I usually changed my clothes and took off my wig before I went home, but I had been right not to do this tonight. I looked out the window for other passengers in love with their drivers, but we were well disguised, we pretended boredom and prayed for traffic. Just as her former home came into view, she made a sudden left turn and asked if I wanted to see where she lived now.

You mean Kate's?

No, that didn't work out. I'm living in this guy I work with's basement.

Sure.

The basement was what is called "unfinished." It was dirt, with a few boards thrown here and there, islands that supported a bed and some milk crates. She waved a flashlight around and said, It's only seventy-five dollars a month.

Really.

Yeah, all this room! It's over fifteen hundred square feet. I can do anything I want with it.

She walked me between the beams, describing her plans. A toilet flushed upstairs, and I could almost see her coworker walking above us. He paused, a couch creaked, a TV was turned on. It was the news. She slipped the flashlight into a hanging loop of string, and a dim spotlight fell on her pillow. I stretched out on the bed and yawned. She stared at the length of me.

You can stay here if you want, I mean if you're tired.

I might just nap.

I have some cleaning up to do.

You clean up, I'll nap.

I listened to her sweeping. She swept closer and closer, she swept all around the edges of the mattress. Then she lay down the broom and climbed into bed with me. We lay there, perfectly still, for a long time. Finally, the man upstairs coughed, which set off a wave of kinetic energy. Pip adjusted her shoulders so that the outermost edge of her T-shirt grazed my arm; I recrossed my legs, carelessly letting my ankle fall against her shin. Five more seconds passed, like heavy bass-drum beats, the three of us were motionless. Then he shifted on the couch and we instantly turned to each other, each mouth fell upon the other, our hands grabbed urgently, even painfully. It seemed necessary to be brutal at first, to mime anger and concede nothing. But once we had wrestled deep into the night and turned out the flashlight, I was surprised by her gentle attentions.

So this was what it was like not to be me. This was who Pip was. Because, make no mistake, I kept my wig on the whole time. I believed it made all of this possible, and I think I was right. The wig and the fact that I did not cry even though I wanted desperately to cry, to tell her how miserable I had been, to squeeze her and make her promise to never leave again. I wanted her to beg me to quit my job and then I wanted to quit my job.

But she didn't beg, and in fact, Mr. Peeps was essential. Each night she picked me up in the Berryman Lumber van, took me under the house, and made love to me. And each morning I went home and took off my wig. I scratched my sweaty scalp and let my head breathe for two hours before getting on the bus to go to work. I lived like this for eight beautiful days. On the ninth day, Pip suggested we go out to breakfast before I went to work.

I wish I could, but I have to go home and get ready.

You look great.

But I have to wash my hair.

Your hair looks great.

I touched my wig and laughed, but she didn't smile.

Really, it looks great.

Our eyes locked, and an unfriendly feeling passed between us. Of course it was a wig—I knew she knew this—but she was suddenly determined to call my bluff. I imagined that we were dueling, delicate foils raised high.

Okay then, let's have breakfast.

I can drop you off at Mr. Peeps after.

Fine. Thank you.

Everyone knows that if you paint a human being entirely with house paint he will live, as long as you don't paint the bottom of his feet. It takes only a little thing like this to kill a person. I had worn the wig for almost thirty hours straight, and as I stripped and jiggled and moaned, I began to feel warm, overly warm. By midday, sweat was running down the sides of my face, but the men just kept coming, it was a day of incredible profits. Allen even patted me on the back as I left, saying, Good work, champ. Pip was waiting in the van, but the walk across the parking lot felt long and strange. I thought I recognized a customer crouching by his car, but no, it was just a normal man huddled over something in a cage. He murmured, That's right, we're going to take you home.

Pip put me right to bed and even borrowed a thermometer from her coworker upstairs. But she did not suggest I take off my wig, and in my fever I understood what this meant. I saw her in the clearing with a pistol and I knew without even looking that my hands were empty. But I could win by pretending to have a pistol. If I said bang and let her shoot me, I would win. If I died this way, as Gwen, would the rest of me still go on living? And what was the rest of me? I fell asleep with this question and tunneled through the night ripping at the knotted strands until the wig came off. I didn't put it on in the morning, and Pip didn't ask how I was feeling; she could see I was fine. She didn't offer to drive me to work, and we both knew she wouldn't be there to pick me up.

I sat in the green plastic chair under the fluorescent lights. It was an extraordinarily slow day. It seemed that all the men in the world were too busy to masturbate. I imagined them out there doing virtuous things, solving crimes and teaching their children how to do cartwheels. It was the last hour of my eight-hour shift, and I had not given a single show. It was almost eerie. I watched the clock and door and began to place bets between them. If no customers came for me in the next fifteen minutes, I would yell Allen's name. Fifteen minutes passed.

Allen!

What.

Nothing.

There were only twenty minutes left now. If no one came in the next twelve minutes, I would yell the word "I," as in me, myself, and. After seven minutes, the door dinged and a man came in. He bought a video and left.

I!

What?

Nothing.

It was the final eight. If no customers came in, I would yell the word "quit." As in no more, enough, I'm going home. I stared at the door. It threatened to open with each breath I took, with each passing minute. One. Two. Three. Four. Five. Six. Seven. Eight.

I Kiss a Door

Now that I know, it seems so obvious. Suddenly, there is
nothing I remember that doesn't contain a clue. I remember
a beautiful blue wool coat with flat silver buttons. It fit her
perfectly, it even gripped her.

Where did you find that coat?

My father bought it for me.

Really? It's so cool.

It just arrived this morning.

He picked it out? How did he know how to pick something so cool?

I don't know.

It seemed unfair that Eleanor should be so pretty and the lead singer of the best band *and* have a dad who sent amazing coats from expensive stores that were tailored to her exact measurements. My father didn't send me anything, but he called me sometimes to ask if I could give him a job.

I'm a waitress.

But what about the person who works under the waitress? The busboy?

Yeah!

We don't have busboys. I bus the tables.

You could subcontract out to me; it would save you a lot of time.

Look, I can't send you money.

Did I ask for money? I asked for work!

I just can't do it right now.

I don't want money; I want a meaningful path in life!

I have to go.

Just fifty dollars. I'll pay the wire fee.

When Shy Panther played at the Lyceum, Eleanor's dad came out to see her, and I got to meet him. He was incredibly handsome, commandingly so. She was mute around him, and to be honest, she seemed less interesting when he was there. Such that when she stepped out on the stage, her tiny presence was almost presumptuous, as in: how had she ever imagined anyone would want to listen to her. She sang,

> *He looks like a door*
> *He tastes like a door*

And when I kiss him
I kiss a door

Her trademark monotone, her famous lack of stage presence—that night they were nothing. She wasn't cool. She was the odd girl in class, forced to recite. I watched her from backstage, standing next to her father, wondering if he was pressing his arm against my arm or if I was imagining it. Yes, I was flirting with him, not just then but all night. He told me something I still tell myself every day. He said: Men are turned on by women who are taller than them. But now I know better, and I preface the sentence with "in heaven." In heaven men are turned on by women who are taller than them. And all the dogs that died are alive again. When the night was over, Eleanor and her dad dropped me off at my apartment and I felt jealous and confused, as if he had chosen her over me. Only it wasn't clear like this, I'm psychoanalyzing with hindsight.

By the time *Thunderheart* came out, I wasn't friends with her anymore. Not because of that night but because I slept with Marshall. He wasn't her boyfriend, I told myself this as I kissed the front of his jeans, but I knew she thought of both the boys in the band as hers. His penis was long and curved down, so that I could fuck him by lying on his back and pulling it up between his legs into me. This sounds impossible, but it's true. You would understand it better if I drew a diagram.

Have you done it like this before? I asked him.

No.

You're lying!

No, I didn't even know it was possible.

So I taught you something! Now you can do it all the time like this.

Yeah. I think it might be the kind of thing that's better for the girl.

Really? Oh God, sorry. Do you want to stop?

Well, are you about to get off or anything?

I think I could.

Okay, that's fine. Take your time.

No, actually, I can't. Let's switch places.

It was Marshall who told me about Eleanor. I hadn't seen him for over a year, and in the meantime I had met Jim, and I think I might have even been pregnant with April. He told me everything while we were standing in the soul aisle of Spillers.

She's living with her parents? Why?

Not her parents, he said, just her dad. They're divorced.

But why? Is she okay?

Well, no, obviously not, since she's living with him.

Is she sick?

No. Did you ever meet her dad?

Yeah, at the Lyceum show.

Then you know about him.

What.

How he's in love with her.

What?

Jesus, you didn't know that?

What?

He divorced her mom to be with her. That's why she lived in Lampeter during high school.

That's not why.

That is why. They lived together as a couple while she went to high school.

I can't believe this. No, she would have told me.

I'm sorry.

Why didn't she tell me?

I'm sorry.

Oh God. She's living with him? Is it like that?

I don't know. No one has talked to her.

But probably, right?

Yeah, probably.

When I bring out the record now, it is like a sword, or a hammer. *Thunderheart*. It is the one amazing piece of evidence of her self. Her very own self, sung in the only voice she had, a voice that she somehow decided was good enough. The band was together for two years; those were the only years she lived on her own, apart from her father. And as far as I know, Marshall and Sal were the only two people she ever told. It is as if she came up from hell to make this one thing, a record, and then she went back. But who am I to say. Maybe it wasn't hell. Maybe she really wanted to go back. Marshall tells me they are still together; they live in Milford Haven. He played a show in Cardiff and she came. When he asked if she was still singing, she laughed and said: Still? You flatter me.

The Boy from Lam Kien

I took twenty-seven steps and then I stopped. Next to the juniper bush. Lam Kien Beauty Salon was before me, and my front door was behind me. It's not agoraphobia, because I am not actually afraid of leaving the house. The fear hits about twenty-seven steps away from the house, right around the juniper bush. I have studied it and determined that it is not a real bush, and I have reversed this theory, and I have done everything I can not to turn around and go home, even if it means standing there forever. I was eating some of the inedible juniper berries when the door of Lam Kien opened and a little boy stepped out. Perhaps Lam Kien's son, Billy Kien. Or maybe Lam Kien was not a name at all but a translation of the words "beauty salon," or "nails 'n' such." Young Kien remained by the door, and I stayed in my twenty-seventh step. He seemed to be waiting for me to move forward. Weren't we all. When it became clear that this was never going to happen, he yelled out to me.

I have a dog!

I nodded. What's his name?

The boy looked sad for a moment, and I realized he did not actually have a dog. I felt honored to be chosen as the person who believed he had a dog. I was the right woman for this job; he had chosen well to choose me. Finally, he yelled out, Paul!, and I dutifully imagined Paul: running with the boy, loving the boy, the boy feeding Paul.

Do you have a dog? Paul's owner asked, walking toward me and stopping in a place where he might get hit by a car.

Don't stand in the street.

He walked over to me, stood before me, did not judge me.

Do you have any pets? he asked.

No.

Not even a cat?

No.

Why not?

I'm not sure I could care for a pet. I travel a lot.

But you could get a very little pet that wasn't very hungry.

I knew all about those things that weren't very hungry; my life was full of them. I didn't want any more weaklings who were activated by water and heat but had no waste and were so small that when they died, I buried them only with forgetfulness. If I was going to bring something new into my home, it would be a big starving thing. But I could not do this. I didn't tell the boy, because I was just his dog-believer.

What kind of pet do you suggest for me?

A tadpole.

But this will grow up to be a frog. I can't have a frog in my house, hopping all over the place.

Oh, no, it won't, it's little! But you'll need an aquarium.

But it will become a frog.

No, it won't! That's another kind of fish.

What kind?

A minnow.

I let it go. Inside me, next to the place where the boy played with his dog, there was now an aquarium holding one tiny tadpole with no appetite. It swam back and forth, feeling perpetually ready to hop, ready for the air on its back, ready for tremendous, fantastic change. It swam forever and Paul never died, but the boy and I were changing even as we stood together. The boy was growing bored and this was a form of growing up. I was getting depressed and this was my own fault. It was a beautiful day and someone was talking to me of his own free will. But I could see the end in sight: the boy's shirt had cartoon characters on it and the cartoon characters were leaning away from me, they were taking a step back as the boy stepped forward. He stood right in front of me and pinched my arm and said, Can I see your room?

Such relief. Even the pinch was good. I understood completely about needing to hurt someone at the same time that you are giving them something. It was wonderful to have an excuse to go home so quickly. As I shut the door behind us, I took a moment to wonder about the law. Laws about showing children your room when you don't know their names. But I did know the name of his imaginary dog. I felt I could say the name Paul without admitting I knew he wasn't real. When the judge told me the boy didn't have a dog, I would act very surprised, disappointed, even hurt. I would cry a little. Perhaps the boy would be sent to jail for lying to me. I looked at his amazing tennis shoes and knew he would be able to handle it. I, on the other hand, have never been able to convincingly wear athletic gear, and prison life would kill me.

He walked around my living room, touching things that had once meant a lot to me but now seemed beside the point. I own many pieces of abstract art. He touched the art with his fingernails. He picked up a book that was lying on the floor and held it in the air between his two fingers. The subtitle of the book was *Keeping Love and Intimacy Alive in Committed Relationships*. I was working through it, word by word. So far I had done Keeping and was just starting on Love. I worried that by the time I got to Committed and Relationships, I would have forgotten Keeping. Not to mention Alive and all the other words. He carried the book like this, between two fingers, into the kitchen. He carefully laid it on the corner of the kitchen floor, and I said thank you and he nodded.

Do you have any eggplant Parmesan?

I said I did not. We moved into the bedroom. He sat on the queen-size bed and kicked off his shoes and then lay back with his arms and legs spread out like a star. I straightened my brush on the dressing table and quietly slid my hair gel in a drawer. I didn't want him to see I was the kind of person who wore hair gel, because I'm not, really. A friend left it here. Wouldn't that be nice? If I had a friend and she brought her hair gel over and she left it here? This is what I would say if I was asked. If he opened the drawer.

You should get bunk beds, then you would have more room, he said while pretending to be sucked down into the narrow space between the bed and the wall.

What would I do with more room?

He now stood, impossibly, between the bed and the wall. A place I had never thought to clean.

You don't want bunk beds?

Well, I just don't see the need for them.

You can have a friend spend the night.

But this bed is so big, they can sleep in here with me.

He gave me a long, strange stare, and my mind bent like a spoon. Why would anyone want to sleep in the bed with me when they could have their own bunk, like on a ship? I asked him if he thought they had bunk beds at Mervyns and he said he thought they did but that I should call first. While I was on hold with Mervyns, he opened the drawer on my dressing table. I blushed. He took out the hair gel and squirted a large amount into his hands and quickly pushed all his shiny black hair straight back and looked in the mirror. He looked like he was standing in a strong wind. We smiled at each other because it was such an incredible look. Mervyns said the bunk beds were only $499. The boy said he thought this was a very reasonable price. He said he would pay a million dollars for bunk beds if he had a million dollars.

We walked back to the front door because he said it was time for him to go. He said this apologetically, as if I would not be able to live without him. I said this was for the best because I had a lot of work to do. When I said "a lot of work," I moved my hands apart to represent all the work. He stared at the space between my palms and asked if I played the accordion. I could feel the accordion between my hands and how impressed he would be if I said yes. I said no, and a pillow fell off the couch by itself. This happens sometimes and I try to ignore it. The boy raised his eyebrows a little and I saw that I was saved. I do not play the accordion or have bunk beds, but I have these pillows. They move by themselves. I opened the door and he left without saying goodbye. I watched him walk across the street to Lam Kien Beauty Salon. He shut the door behind him. I shut my door and listened to the sucking sound. It was the sound of Earth hurtling away from the apartment at a speed too fast to imagine. And as all of creation pulled away in this tornado-like vortex, it laughed—the sarcastic laugh of something that has never had to *try*. I peeked out the window. Beyond the juniper bush, there was just gray smoke swirling in every direction. I shut the curtains so that they overlapped. I walked around the apartment. I stared at the book in the corner of the kitchen floor. I put the cap back on the hair gel. The covers on my bed were all messed up. I ran my hand over the topography of the bedspread. There were river valleys and mountain communities. There was smooth desert tundra. There was a city, and in that city, there was a beauty salon. I took off my shoes and got under the covers. I whispered, Shut your eyes, and I shut my eyes and pretended it was night and that the world was all around me, sleeping. I told myself that the sound of my breathing was really the sound of all the animals in the world breathing, even the humans, even the boy, even his dog, all together, all breathing, all on Earth, at night.

Making Love in 2003

She had a needlepoint pillow that read: MAKING LOVE IN 2002.
On the other side of the couch there was MAKING LOVE IN
1997, in blue, with a ruffle around the edge. I guessed there
were more, but I tried not to look for them. I didn't want to
see the one with the current year on it. Or if there wasn't
one, I didn't want to know why. She asked me polite questions, and we waited for her husband.

He says you're very talented, are you self-taught?

Yes, I'm really just beginning, though. I have so much to
learn.

Well, it sounds like you're off to a good start.

Thank you.

After a while it seemed she was growing a little angry, with him for not being there and with me for being there. It occurred to me that if he didn't appear soon, I would have to leave. My heart fell because I hadn't planned anything for my future beyond this meeting. I had written every day for a year with his business card taped to my computer, and now I was done and he had said to call him when I was done and I had, I had called, and now the ball was in his court. It was his job to do with me what he would. What would he do? What do the men do with the very talented young women who have finished writing their books? Would he kiss me? Would he invite me to be his daughter or wife or babysitter? Would he send me and my book to the place where the next thing would happen? Would he rub my legs and let me cry? His wife and I waited to find out. She had less patience than me. I was willing to wait forever, and she was giving him five more minutes. We waited out the five minutes in silence, and then she stood and said, Well. I looked up at her and smiled. I pretended I was from another country and couldn't read her body language. She pressed her lips together and looked down at her hands.

He probably already called your house to reschedule.

I nodded, but I knew that he hadn't called my house because I had moved everything out of my house and put it in my car, which was parked out in front of his house. I was all ready to go. There was no point in rescheduling. I could

wait in the car or wait in the house, but I had nothing else
to do. I preferred to wait in the house.

You can just do whatever you would normally do if I
wasn't here, I said.

She looked at me, wondering if she had ever met anyone
as stupid. I didn't care. It wasn't her card taped to my computer, sitting in the backseat of my car.

I would normally be writing, she said. I doubted this, but
maybe it was true. Maybe she would be writing a letter to
her sister or writing the word "sweaters" on a big box of
sweaters before putting it in the attic for the summer.

What are you writing?

It's a sequel to a book I wrote a few years ago.

Oh. What was the first book called?

A Swiftly Tilting Planet.

She said this gently, politely, knowing I would have heard
of it. I stood and felt pains in my legs. I hadn't planned on
standing again until he got here, but now here I was, standing beside Madeleine L'Engle, the famous author. I looked
around the living room. This was Madeleine L'Engle's living
room. MAKING LOVE IN 2002. MAKING LOVE IN 1997. There
were probably piles of these pillows in every room of the
house, dating back to the sixties. I looked at her tailored
brown pants and realized he was probably making love to her
right this second. When you reach a certain saturation point,
lovemaking becomes one endless vibration. He was running
late, and this was a way of making love to her, and she wanted
to write but had to entertain me instead, and this was her
way of making love to him. I was just a part of the lovemak-

ing between Madeleine L'Engle and her husband. A tiny part of MAKING LOVE IN 2003. My plans were not well thought out, this was suddenly very clear. I told her I had really enjoyed *A Swiftly Tilting Planet* and looked forward to the sequel. She thanked me and said she was sure he would call if he hadn't already. She walked me out to the porch. There was my car. We looked at my car. It had many things in it, and some of them were sticking out of the trunk. She shook my hand, and I walked toward the car and wished that I could walk toward the car forever, with this confidence about where I was headed. I was headed to the car.

It doesn't really feel like driving when you don't know where you're going. There should be an option on the car for driving in place, like treading water. Or at least a light that shines between the brake lights that you can turn on to indicate that you have no destination. I felt like I was fooling the other drivers and I just wanted to come clean. But the more I drove, the more I felt like I had somewhere to go. I was making difficult left turns that no one would ever do unless they had to. Sometimes I would make left turns all the way around a block, and when I returned to the original intersection, I would feel disappointed to find all the drivers were new. It wasn't like a square dance, where you miraculously end up with your original partner, laughing and feeling giddily relieved to find him after dancing with everyone else in the world. Instead, they swung around and kept on going, some people were at work by now, or halfway to the airport. In fact, driving might be the thing most opposite of dancing. I wondered if I would spend the rest of my life inventing complicated ways to depress myself, now that I had finished my book and gone to meet the man who said I had promise a year ago but wasn't home today.

What most people would do in my situation is go to their boyfriend's house. They would go there and cry and be handed tissues and cry some more and never stop to think that they should really be laughing and smiling joyfully because their boyfriend is an actual physical being on the same plane of reality as them. I know what I'm talking about here, I wrote a whole book on this subject that Madeleine L'Engle's husband once said had promise. Now it is the last thing I want to write about, so I will give you the short version here.

When I was fifteen, a dark shape came into my room at night. It was dark, but it glowed, which is the first of many facts you will have to tackle with your imagination. It wasn't in the shape of a person, but right away I knew it was like a person in every way except for how it looked. As it turns out, our looks are not the main thing that makes us human.

I knew right away it was a sexual predator because it was vibing me and I felt self-conscious in my nightgown, which was really just a big T-shirt. This is why you should wear underwear to bed. I was scared, but not in the way where you decide you would rather die than move or breathe. I kept my eyes on the shape and made a plan to jump out of bed and grab my jeans, which were on the floor. This was before I knew anything about anything, for instance that all human movement is in slow motion compared to how fast you can move if you are just a glowing darkness. I had only lifted my hand a little bit when the darkness was upon me. This is the part I stretched out over a whole chapter because I knew Madeleine L'Engle's husband would get off on it. Basically, what happened was that it fucked me. It did this by entering my body with its whole self. All of the darkness was inside me, and I could feel it glowing, like the volume of music when it shows you how to move. Just the weekend before, I had danced in a sexy way for the first time; my butt and the beat had connected in a way that portended great things in my future. But I didn't think it would happen so soon, and like this. Later, I realized my dance moves were probably so powerful, they had called it from its corner of the universe. I'm not saying I asked for it, only that there are moments when we are sending signals not just to the boys in the room but to all of creation.

It has been suggested that I invented the story of the dark shape to cope with the pain of a more earthly rapist. If that theory interests you, I can recommend some great case studies about girls who did that, lied. If I was scared the first time, it was because I didn't know I could survive such pleasure. I thought maybe I was trading my life for this. To feel my teenage desire escalate to inhuman proportions. To look down on my own body and know that falling would mean dying not just once but many times. To fall for a million years like a flute falls, musically, played by the air it is passing through. And to land with no mind, but with a heart that was breaking. We cuddled afterward, and I was coy and shy. I passed my hand through its densities, asking if that hurt but knowing nothing I did could hurt it, I could only drive it crazy. Occasionally, it would seep back into me, and then I would sleep a bit and awaken with fear that it was gone. But there it was, cloaked around me, healing my appendectomy scar more completely than I could manage myself.

What else can you do?

Love you.

But can you do any more tricks?

No.

But I'm the only one, right?

You are the sweetest thing in the universe.

I am?

Yeah, by a long shot.

My disposition was that of all the girls who dated boys from other high schools. We were barely there. Our feelings could not be hurt because they lay elsewhere, off-campus, aurora borealis. I drew pictures of it on my binder, a smudge in a heart. A smudge and me in interconnecting hearts. Me and the smudge and a half-human/half-smudge baby. Before I went to bed, I put on makeup, and in the early years, I wore cute nightgowns, but by the end of high school, I just threw myself down on my bed, naked, waiting. Our conversations happened in my blood, or if I wanted to hear its voice, I could hold down F-sharp and middle C on my plastic Casio, and from underneath these notes came a far-off staticky voice, like a truck driver on CB, just out of range. There was a horrible longing inside this love. It would suck on my nipples, and my mouth would swell with thirst, I wanted to suck, too. I became convinced that having me was better than what I got. Now I know this wasn't true, but you have to remember I was still technically a virgin. I had never even kissed anyone.

This story ends in college, when I became angry and dismissive and wanted a real boyfriend. The dark shape wept in the incredibly sad way that only air can cry, and I had tremendous empathy, but only for myself. I was pretty sure the relationship was committing crimes against my brand-new feminism, and underneath that was a determined curiosity about this thing called cock. The shape did the only thing it could do: it promised to come to me in human form. It would be a man named Steve.

Will you date me when I ask you out? it asked.

Yes.

Even if I'm ugly and you don't like my personality?

Yes.

No, you won't.

I will!

You're just saying that because you're in a hurry.

Well, it won't be my fault if I miss the bus.

Goodbye, sweetness.

Bye! Where's my backpack?

It's on the counter.

Oh. Bye!

About a year later, I did meet a man named Steve. He was the dad of a friend of mine, and he was dying of cancer. I helped her minister to him for two months. Sometimes, when she left the room, I would lean against his bed and whisper hi and he would whisper hi and I would hold his hand and we would stay like this for a little while. He wasn't my dark shape. But when I rubbed his dying arms, I felt something tremendously fast in them, a gathering of speed. So much of him was already quick, and yet he still had to die in obscenely slow motion because this is what humans do. In his last days, I held vigil with my friend, both of us lost in despair, playing records we thought he might like, but who really knew for sure. What a terrible mistake to let go of something wonderful for something real. After Steve died, I stopped being friends with his daughter and moved out of the dorms. When I began to write, it was out of fear. I thought I might forget, or pretend to forget, or pretend to pretend, or grow up. What my college adviser, Madeleine L'Engle's husband, eventually called a promising piece of fiction had started out as evidence. One day I would hand this manuscript over, and Steve would nod and say yes, F-sharp, yes, middle C, yes, you have found me at last, come sit on my lap, sweetness.

I thought maybe I would swing by Madeleine's house and see if his car was out front. It was either this or begin a career as something other than a writer. If I thought of another career before I got to the house, I would turn around and pursue that. I made the car go slowly so that everyone could see it was thinking. It was considering careers for me. I looked out the windows and tried to see who the pedestrians thought I was when they looked at my car. But they didn't look at my car; they looked inward. They considered themselves and their own cars; they made love with their hurrying. They took each step as if it would not be their last, and it wasn't. They did not look up and stare into my headlights and whisper, "special-needs assistant," and thus, when I rounded the corner of Madeleine's block, I was still planning on being a writer.

There was his car. But it came early; it was parked in front of a house at the other end of the block from his own. Maybe everybody else knows what this means. My first thought was Alzheimer's disease, and I worried for myself and my career in the hands of this man who couldn't remember where his own house was. It had been a year since I'd graduated, obviously long enough for his life to go to pieces. Madeleine must have to do everything for him. Oh, Madeleine. And he was sitting in the car. I had heard of this, Alzheimer's patients who return to their pre–combustion-engine minds and cannot remember how to open the door. As I walked toward him, I could feel my new career take hold. I was the nurse of Madeleine L'Engle's husband. With my help, she would have enough time to write the sequel. I was everything a good daughter should be, except I was paid. It was wonderful to be needed; I was headed toward the car.

At first I thought he had a cat in his lap, and then I saw it was Theresa Lodeski. We were both in Early Chinese Philosophical Texts junior year. She hadn't graduated, but now I could see that, in a way, she had. Theresa Lodeski was very, very pretty, but she had an identical twin sister, Pauline, who was somehow infinitely prettier than her. If you lined up their faces and tried to locate the difference, feature by feature, you couldn't find it. But everybody knew. The only reason to look at Theresa was to check to see if she was Pauline. When she wasn't, you looked away; when she was, you looked a little longer. This was definitely Theresa; she had come into her own.

I should have left the second I saw he didn't have Alzheimer's. But I had a tingling in my arms. I was an angel

116

looking down into the world, into one car on the world, into two members of mankind, into their souls, and into the place behind their souls: the void. She looked up, our eyes clicked, she remembered me from Early Chinese Philosophical Texts. Madeleine L'Engle's husband opened his mouth. I could tell he was about to use one of the five question words: who, what, why, where, or when.

What?

That woman.

What woman?

She's gone now.

Did she see us?

Yeah. She was in Early Chinese Philosophical Texts.

What?

We were in a class together.

Are you fucking with me? You knew her?

I should probably go.

Fuck! This is fucked! Did she see me?

No. I'm going now.

Is she still out there?

No, she's gone.

How does anyone ever let go of anything? My book was a long glove clasping the dark shape I had loved. Inside the glove was one very pale young hand that had never learned to grip skin. It was so raw it looked wet. I fell into the eyes of every person I passed on the street. Food seemed impossibly strange. Children thought I was a child and tried to play with me, but I could neither play nor work, I could only wonder why. Why do people live at all. I read every single ad in the classifieds section each week. Real Estate, Employment, Counseling, Home Services, Getaways, Musicians Market, Dating, Women and Men Seeking Each Other and Themselves, Chance Meetings, and Automotive. I had narrowed it down to either *Power trio seeks excellent 2nd guitar for heavy rock* or *Angela Mitchell LCSW, therapy supporting the integration of body, mind, spirit, and world.* I settled on Angela Mitchell because the power trio wanted an experienced gigger, and I wasn't sure what that was. But as I rose in the elevator toward Angela's office, I whispered the words "experienced gigger" to myself, and they calmed me. I hoped Angela Mitchell meant her ad literally. I imagined a couples counseling/séance for me and the dark shape.

But when I was sitting in her big soft chair, staring at an abstract print of orange circles inside of oranger circles, I found that I was mute. When she finally asked why I had come, I said I had broken up with my boyfriend over a year ago and still regretted it. She bludgeoned me with a look of such limitless compassion that I immediately began to cry. I wondered briefly if she might adopt me or hire me as her assistant or become my lesbian lover. I blew my nose, and she asked if I had ever seen the musical *South Pacific.*

I think I saw it on TV once.

Do you remember the scene where the women are washing their hair?

No.

They sang a little song, do you remember what it was?

No.

"I'm Going to Wash That Man Right Out of My Hair."

Oh.

Do you understand what I am saying?

I think so.

Is there anything else you want to talk about?

Well, I've been thinking maybe I should get a job. Do you think I should?

Definitely.

The special-needs assistant helps the special-needs teacher who teaches the children with special needs. Buckman was in transition when they hired me. Originally, it had been a school for kids with all different disabilities, but now the kids with physical challenges, the kind you can see, were sent to Logan Education Center. Logan had amazing play structures for students in wheelchairs, and "soft rooms" where those same students were taken out of their wheelchairs and encouraged to do free body movement. They were reminded that movement is about more than just getting from A to B, it is nuance and emotion, and they were the inventors of New Gesture. Once a month they were visited by a group of researchers from Microsoft. The researchers would take off their shoes and lie on the floor and just let it all happen around them. Apparently, this is how the computer touch pad was invented. Every week we heard stories about Logan, and it made me and my students feel as though we were not on the cutting edge. We were slow readers, and speed-readers with no comprehension, we were too nervous to learn, too happy to learn, too angry to learn; learning seemed beside the point.

The older students were allowed to keep their orange bottles of Ritalin and Adderall in their desks, and legally, they could raise their hands and ask to be excused for almost anything. The side effects of Ritalin are headaches, anxiety, sleep disorder, irritability, depression, gastrointestinal upset, and the jitters. I was assigned to the ones who needed extra help with their reading skills. I knew where I was headed: to the bottom of each page and the top of the next. I felt like I could do this forever, because nothing mattered more than anything else. I was patience defined, patience misspelled, patience sounded out slowly, letter by letter, with the *t* pronounced "shh."

In the spring a special-education school called Obley shut down because of asbestos, and Buckman had to absorb all the Obley students and teachers. We had extra room because of the students who had left for Logan, but it was still a nightmare. The kids adapted easily, but the teachers resented one another like in-laws. We were all sure our way was the right way, and there were endless petitions hanging on clipboards in the staff kitchen, mobilizations *against* lining up before the bell, or *for* cursive. I was for cursive. I wrote my name on the pro-cursive clipboard. I left the kitchen and walked back to my room. I tidied the teacher's desk and wrote PUEBLO on the chalkboard. I held my breath as I drew the O. I drew it slowly, oh so slowly. There was a knock at the classroom door. The O was done. I put down my chalk and walked to the door. Oh, the pounding heart. Oh, the held breath. Oh, how did I know. I opened the door. He had sandy brown hair and was taller than me. His face was an animal face, a cat-giraffe face that said everything in the absence of language. His clothes were careless and perfect, just areas that loosely mapped his nakedness. He said he was sorry he was late, and I said, Well, you're here now, and I hugged him and his darkness swelled around me for an instant and whispered, Hello, sweetness into my blood. He pulled away, the teenager pulled away, but his eyes held my eyes like hands. He gave me a note.

Dear Teacher,

Please excuse Steven Krause for his absence. He contracted bronchitis during his last week at Obley and was not well enough to join Buckman with the other students in April. He is well now and will make up any missed work.

Thank you,
Marilyn Krause

He was not swift of mind, why should he be. He was a blur. He was a teenager needing me, as I had been a teenager needing him. And so I helped him. I sat beside his desk, and together we pushed through paragraphs, painstakingly sounding out the words, knitting them into human sentences that said very little. Suddenly, it seemed that language was nothing at all. Saying, *You were my phantom lover* would clarify nothing. I had already tried this, of course, right away. I brought in my book, the one that did not lead to a career in writing, and I sat nervously at his side as he sounded out the entire prologue, all the disclaimers and claimers and dedications to him, my dark shape. My gorgeous, pubescent, and mildly autistic onetime lover, lover-to-be.

I'm going to ask you a few questions to test your comprehension, okay?

Okay.

Is the book a true story?

Yes. No, wait—no! No.

It *is* a true story.

Oh, that's what I thought, but then I thought it might be a trick question.

No, these are all real questions.

Okay.

So when the author says, "When I was fifteen, a dark shape came into my room at night," who is she talking about? Who is the dark shape?

Who?

Yeah. Is it her father? Is it you? Who is it?

Ummmmmumumum. I don't think we know yet at this part of the book.

You're right, we don't.

That was kind of a trick question.

I'm sorry.

And so there was a kind of divide. I knew him, and somewhere deep inside, he knew me, too, and it was up to me, as the special-needs assistant, to remind him. I saw myself as a kind of Anne Sullivan figure. There would be a breakthrough moment, like when Anne pumped the water on Helen Keller's face and Helen spelled the word "water" on Anne's hand, first slowly and then faster and faster, laughing and crying. Anne Sullivan wrote of this moment: *Suddenly I felt a misty consciousness as of something forgotten—a thrill of returning thought; and somehow the mystery of language was revealed to me.* Only it wasn't the mystery of language we needed revealed, it was mystery itself, before language, still draped in the mists. I saw the darkness swirling inside him. I saw that his feet did not touch the ground when he played basketball at recess. In moments, he was flying. Not like a bird but subtly, like a person.

Of course, there was only so much I could do as the special-needs assistant. One thing I could do was pray. I prayed while I looked into his eyes, and my prayer was Hello, hello, hello. Sometimes I heard my shape reply, and I had to press my knuckles against my thighs to keep them near me and away from the boy. The boy, who himself was so compelling in the way boys can be. How he pushed his hair off his sweaty forehead, the mineral smell of him, his hand holding a pencil, holding a pencil, holding a pencil, his hand! Our old affair was so easy, it was the dream that lovers have of consuming each other entirely. Now there was this extra thing, the boy, and the feeling I had carving into my gut, the feeling of wanting to fuck him, as he had fucked me when I was fifteen—into other galaxies.

I began to think this was as close as I could get to him, the shape. So after a while, I did not try very hard to help him read. I decided that reading was the wrong direction for our relationship. Not everyone has to be literate, there are some great reasons for resisting language, and one of them is love. The boy's disability was the shape's way of saying, I love you,

I am here, it is me. I tried to be satisfied with this, and in the meantime, the boy himself began to love me. This was terribly, horribly, wonderfully sweet. It was, I supposed, the thing I had missed out on in high school. He would look at me and look away and look back again and look away and break the tip of his pencil and say fuck and blush and look at my leg and then look at the floor. A long hard look at the linoleum floor, in which he no doubt saw other things, the tits and spread ass of his young teacher and what he would do to them. Have I ever adored anything as much as I adored the sight of him glancing down at his own boner to see if it was hidden by the desk. It was.

There is only one way this ever happens. The student is walking home from school, and the teacher drives by and asks if he wants a ride. The boy looks at his teacher. The sun is shining into his eyes and he squints, and there is a pause wherein the shining of the sun and the squinting of the boy are the only two movements on earth. Even the birds stop. The teacher is momentarily paralyzed by the squinting and shining, but it is not enough to save the boy. She leans across the car and unlocks the passenger door, and with this movement the boy's youngness ends and he becomes old.

Should I take you home?

Whatever's fine.

Do you have to be home at a certain time?

No.

Is there somewhere you'd like to go?

Well, we could park.

For the first six months I just walked around in a constant

state of amazement. I looked at other couples and wondered how they could be so calm about it. They held hands as if they weren't even holding hands. When Steve and I held hands, I had to keep looking down to marvel at it. There was my hand, the same hand I've always had—oh, but look! What is it holding? It's holding Steve's hand! Who is Steve? My three-dimensional boyfriend. Each day I wondered what would happen next. What happens when you stop wanting, when you are happy. I supposed I would go on being happy forever. I knew I would not mess things up by growing bored. I had done that once before.

There were a few complications. There was the fact that he didn't know we had dated previously. As it turned out, this didn't matter. Loving is all in the blood anyway. He called the feeling between us "weird," and I had nothing to add. I kissed the backs of his legs and they sang. He reached around and pulled me down onto his back and I lay there, like on the warm sand of a beach. Just that. That is all there is. That is the whole point of everything.

There was also the issue of our age difference. When you are dating someone much younger, you start to notice other couples with the same issue. You meet people who are dating people fifteen or even twenty years older or younger. You get to talking.

I think it's a turn-on.

Oh, me, too. I would never date a guy my age, they have to be at least ten years younger.

Steve is ten years younger than me. I think he likes it that I'm older.

Of course he does. All guys fantasize about older women. It's a mom thing.

Yeah, but thank God I'm younger than his mom.

I'm not. Gabe's mom is forty.

Oh. How old are you?

Forty-three. How old are you?

Twenty-four.

We learned to be discreet. It helped that nobody really cares about anyone but themselves anyway. They check to make sure you aren't killing anyone, anyone they know, and then they go back to what they were saying about how they think they might be having a real breakthrough in their relationship with themselves. People are always breaking through, like in the Doors song "Break on Through (To the Other Side)." But I really had. I had broken through twice now, and my feeling about the universe was that it was porous and radical and you could turn it on, you could even fuck around with the universe. And this whole time I was still the special-needs assistant. I was helping kids right and left. I was tapping in to their essential energies and leading them, if not into literacy, at least toward eventual pleasure. I wanted all of them to know love one day. I wanted the girls to pull their shoulders back and walk fearlessly into darkness. I wanted the boys to settle down a little. There was a group of boys in the back who never paid attention. They passed notes that weren't even folded into the smallest possible square. Notes floated across the back row like large white sailboats. It was completely infuriating and made me want to humiliate them until they would never dare pass such a big note again. Why else was folding invented? I lurched toward the back of the room and grabbed the first sail I saw. It wasn't even folded in half once. It said: *Caitlin gives Steve K. head.*

Maybe it should have been a relief that it wasn't my name. It wasn't a relief. My breathing reversed itself. I was completely unprepared for this moment. My thighs disintegrated into waves of contractions, and suddenly I understood why people liked guns. Not to shoot, God no, I'm a total pacifist, but just to *have.* To know that it is there. If there had been a gun in my drawer, I could have thought of it now and it would have calmed me. I would have taken a deep breath and scolded the boys. But because there was no gun, I walked over to Caitlin's desk. I looked into the circle of her face and asked her to please step into the hallway. It was difficult to shape air so precisely, into those exact sounds. She rose and walked ahead of me across the room. When I passed by Steve, he looked down like a fifteen-year-old boy who is in trouble with his teacher. Caitlin and I stood in the hall. It smelled like wax and old bananas.

Do you give Steve head?

Steve who?

Steve K.

Oh. I thought you meant the other Steve.

Steve Gonzales?

Yeah.

No. Are you his girlfriend?

Steve Gonzales's? No.

I meant Steve K.

Oh. Yeah. We go out.

Her hair was in two French braids, and she was wearing a sweatshirt that said TOMMY GIRL. She wasn't even afraid of me. She asked where I got my earrings and I said my aunt gave them to me for Christmas and she said she hadn't gotten shit for Christmas and then we walked back to the classroom. I didn't look at Steve. I didn't know if he had made the first move or if the dark shape had a thing for teenage girls, or even what I was really talking about when I said the words "dark shape" to myself. I pressed my hot face against the chalkboard for a few seconds and then I wrote the word PEACE. That is the only good thing about being the special-needs assistant. You can write "peace" on the chalkboard any time you want. Who could complain? It was peace. It can only ever help to write it.

This morning I woke up to the sound of the neighbor trimming his tree. I told myself he would stop trimming only if I got out of bed. The tree got smaller and smaller. Soon it was just a stump, and he had to go underground and start trimming the roots, and still I couldn't get up. The roots were gone and he was sawing through the earth and I told myself that when he came out in China, I would get up. It took him all day. I wept and curled and uncurled myself in a way I couldn't control. I was actually writhing in heartache, as if I were a single muscle whose purpose was to mourn. But by the time my neighbor hit the molten core, I was motionless. I had exhausted myself into a blank stare, a full-body examination of the ceiling. I could feel him pushing up underneath the streets of Shanghai, and to my horror, I felt hunger. The body's expression of hope. As he burst through the ground and into the Chinese air, I sat up. He plowed into the sky, upward through tree leaves and then the clouds. My neighbor sawed into outer space. He cut through the Milky Way, right through the stars and stardust. He went around the universe in a giant circle. And then he landed, with a quiet thud, back in his yard. I lifted the curtain and saw him putting out the sprinkler. It was dusk. If he saw me, I would live. Look up, look up, look up. He raised his eyes, as if it were his own idea, and I waved.

Note: Although Madeleine L'Engle did write a book called *A Swiftly Tilting Planet,* the character who bears her name in this story is a complete fiction, as is the character of her husband.

Ten True Things

Some of those women are really good sewers and you won-der, Why are they taking a beginning sewing class? I like to think it's because they have low self-esteem. They seem totally in control and born to make the rest of us feel clumsy, but inside, they have an almost psychotically warped vision of themselves. At least I am in touch with my skill level. I am a really bad sewer. Interestingly, though, I am not the worst in the class; the tiny Asian woman next to me is. I was sure she would be a really good sewer because most of the clothes in the world are made by Asian women, and also, who's going to be better at making a kimono, me or someone who is Chinese or Japanese. Boy, did she teach me a thing or two about racial prejudice. Is she even trying to make a kimono-style robe, or does she think we are making dog beds? I used to get incredibly distracted by her; I was just so amazed at her interpretation of the directions. Like the teacher would say, Trim the excess cloth, and the woman would carefully fold her pink flannel in half, pin it, and then sit back, waiting for the next instruction. What happens when you do the exact opposite of everything you are told? How would she know when she was done? And why wasn't anyone doing anything about this? Should I do something? What should I do? But then one day the teacher came around and told me to rip out my last five seams and I wanted to yell, *My* seams? At least my seams are for bipeds, what about her last five seams? Right then, as if she was reading my mind, the teacher put her hand on the woman's shoulder and said, Sue, you are such an artist. And Sue laughed and the teacher laughed and they laughed together. So whatever. Obviously, I don't know anything about anything. It doesn't matter, because I'm not even taking this class to learn how to sew. I have my own personal reason for being here.

He thinks I don't know anything about computers, but I know enough to know he spends all day e-mailing. I know the difference between a spreadsheet and Eudora. He doesn't even turn down the sound on the computer, so all day I overhear the "you have mail" tone. And I have to pretend it's the sound of math. I can tell when he's gotten a good one, a sex one, because he gets all loose and casual with me, to counteract the raging of his heart. I am not being poetic here, I can see it pounding, moving the pocket of his shirt. I know this man, I am the neck he breathes down. I am his secretary.

He used to rent two offices, his own and a tiny one for me. But then he said things were getting tight and we should share an office. Tight. He adds thirteen to seventy-two. Two plus three is five, check the e-mail, one plus seven is, check the e-mail, eight, check the e-mail, which comes to a total of, who the hell am I anyway, eighty-five. This is how he dismembers his day, in the most painful way, moment by moment. A bigger man would just shoot it, put it out of its misery. Or a better accountant might actually account for something instead of hiring another, slightly cheaper accountant to do the accounting, and skidding by on the difference. You act surprised, but surely you know. Accountants do this all the time, and so do Indian restaurants. Sag paneer? Very good choice. The waiter hands the order to the cook, the cook hands it to the busboy, the busboy runs down the block and orders sag paneer from the other Indian restaurant, the shoddy one, takeout. This is why the more expensive restaurants take longer to bring out the food. It's all that running. In this case, I am the busboy, I am the one who hires the real accountant, I spare him the indignity. Why would someone do this, go through all the trouble of pretending to be an accountant when it would be so much easier to not be one. Because you get bound in, you say you will and then you have to and then they expect you to and it just seems easier to do it. I think he told her he was an accountant on their first date.

Then he got business cards made that said RICK MARASOVIC, ACCOUNTANT, 236-4954, and he handed her one. Then he got a phone, for the number, then a desk, for the phone, then an office, for the desk, and then me. So in a sense, we are both working for her.

I wanted to know who she was. Was she terrifyingly beautiful? Was she so ignorant she didn't deserve the truth? Was she also a liar and thus it was something they did together? I don't believe in psychology, which says everything you do is because of yourself. That is so untrue. We are social animals, and everything we do is because of other people, because we love them, or because we don't. She never came to the office, but she called sometimes. Usually, he'd tell me to tell her he wasn't in.

Rick Marasovic's office.

Dana, it's Ellen.

Hi, Ellen.

(Rick nods, yes, he's in, or shakes his head, no, he's not.)
Is Rick in?

No, he's not. Can I take a message?

Can you ask him to pick up my flower essences on the way home?

What's a flower essence?

It's a type of medicine made out of distilled flowers.

Like rose water?

Well, in this case, it's pink monkeyflower.

What's it medicine for?

Overcoming body shame.

Oh. I'll tell him.

(Or another time)

Hi, is Rick in?

No, he's not. Can I take a message?

Can you tell him to call me as soon as possible?

Where's the fire?

What?

What's the hurry?

I'm at loose ends.

Oh. I'll tell him.

Thus, over the years, I came to know her. Not the way I knew him; I didn't watch the minute tides of her sweat roll in and out over the course of each day. But, like ivy, we grow where there is room for us. She seemed to have room for me; she never turned away in the pauses that allow for turning away. She never inquired, but she never recoiled, either. This is a quality that I look for in a person, not recoiling. Some people need a red carpet rolled out in front of them in order to walk forward into friendship. They can't see the tiny outstretched hands all around them, everywhere, like leaves on trees.

Rick Marasovic's office.

Dana, it's Ellen.

Hi, Ellen.

Is Rick in?

He just stepped out. Can I take a message?

Can you tell him I'll be home late?

Why so late?

I have a beginning sewing class.

Where?

At the Adult Education Center.

Oh. I'll tell him.

It was a hand outstretched, a woman's dry open palm, and I clasped it. I went home early to study my apartment before the class. I wanted to look at everything through her eyes. I do this before I bring someone new into my life; I try to get a sense of who I am so that I can make it easier for them to know me. I walked around the apartment, looking through the eyes of someone who had body shame and an interest in sewing. I moved some things around in the kitchen and threw my best sweater carelessly across my bed. I dusted the television but messed up the papers on my desk. She wouldn't come here, but I would return to this place after having met her, and I knew I would appreciate my forethought.

It was not immediately obvious who Ellen was because we did not play any name games at the start of the class. Past a certain age, they give up on the name games, which is regrettable for someone like me who loves anything that involves going around a circle and saying something about yourself. I wish there was a class where we could just keep going around the circle, around and around, until we had finally said everything about ourselves. This class was in rows, so it was hard to see all the faces. There were fourteen Singer Scholastic sewing machines, and we each sat in front of one. Somehow I had not anticipated the machines; I had imagined a needle and thread, women sitting around sewing and chatting. I guess that's more like a quilting bee. But when the teacher came around to watch each of us sew a straight line, I listened carefully, and the soft brown head in front of me murmured that she was having trouble threading the bobbin, with "threading the bobbin" said like "pink monkeyflower" had been said. A dear brown head, soft brown hair, dear dear hair, dear soft head. At work the next day, I looked at him newly, I tried to see some grace in him, something that such softness could land on. Maybe it was there, maybe it was, and I just couldn't see it from my point of view as a person who, more or less, hated him.

The next weekend I bought red and blue plaid at Fabric Depot, and as I was leaving the store, she was walking toward it from her car. I paused and then realized she wouldn't recognize me because I had sat behind her in class. So I let her go. I watched her walk into the store as unself-consciously as an animal in a nature documentary. In class the next day, she pulled out the most breathtaking fabric. It had pictures of feathers, all the different kinds of feathers from all the different kinds of birds on earth. And from where I was sitting, they looked photographic. Can they do that? Put photos on flannel? I imagined her flying around the world, taking photographs of all the birds, them flocking around her, them teaching her to fly, her flying through the air on her back, totally unafraid. She was still having the trouble with the bobbin this week, as I was. Sue took out her bobbin entirely and set it on the floor. Bobbinless and with great confidence. That Sue.

Ellen turned to me first. It often happens this way,

because I am large. Smaller things flow toward larger things, and in the case of oceans and rivers, the smaller thing becomes one with the larger thing. We did not become one, but we introduced ourselves after class, and I said I was her husband's secretary. I told her she had inspired me to take the same class, and that I hoped we could know each other. It's important to build friendships on honesty. She nodded and was completely darling in every way. I'm not talking about lesbianism here, though I don't object to that, and I suppose I could be seduced if a woman did a particularly slow, skilled striptease in front of me in candlelight with subtle body contact. I'm open to new things, but this wasn't like that. We went back to my apartment after this second class. I gave her a tour, and when she peeked into my bedroom, her eyes fell on my best sweater, which I had rethrown across the bed each day. She said, How cozy, and a feeling of coziness encircled us. When she saw my messy desk, she said she was the same way, and there was no dust on the TV, and I was easy to love. People just need a little help because they are so used to not loving. It's like scoring the clay to make another piece of clay stick to it.

I made orange juice from concentrate and showed her the trick of squeezing the juice of one real orange into it. It removes the taste of being frozen. She marveled at this, and I laughed and said, Life is easy. What I meant was, Life is easy with you here, and when you leave, it will be hard again. The day felt like a birthday, our first, and we ourselves were the gifts, to be opened again and again. One thing we did was try on each other's shoes. My shoes were almost twice as big as hers, and this seemed okay. It wasn't just my shoes; it was my feet and all the other parts of my body, too. She held her arm against my arm, and it looked like an embryo next to a child. She said maybe she was still growing, and we pressed our legs against each other's legs, and these, too, were radically different sizes, and our curiosity was blossoming like a rose, we wanted to know, we really wanted to know, all the unknowable things about each other and how we were the same and how we were different, if we even were, maybe nobody is. We wanted to strike lightning in dark waters, to see, if only for a second, the entire world that lives down there, the ten million species in amazing colors and patterns; show us life, now. We pressed our stomachs and lips together, and these, too, were different sizes, but my lips were roughly the same size as her ear, and her arm, when wrapped around my waist, felt long and, more important, was warm. We grew still and stared at each other. It seemed incredibly dangerous to look into each other's eyes, but we were doing it. For how long can you behold another person? Before you have to think of yourself again, like dipping the brush back in for more ink. For a very long time; you didn't need to get more ink, there was no reason to get anything else, because she was as good as me, she lived on earth like me, she suffered as I did. It was she who looked away and pulled the sheet to her chin.

After this I poured more orange juice and showed her how to make orange juice ice cubes. But she said she already knew how to make those. She put on her skirt and tiny shoes. Suddenly, it was very late, and from where I was sitting, I could see the dust starting to reunite on the TV. I would probably never dust the TV again; I wouldn't have a reason to. This made me feel so violently sad that I got a cloth and began dusting it right then and there, and as I did, she said, Can I ask you a personal question? I said, What? And she said, Would you ever touch a woman? I paused in my dusting. This wasn't a question, it was an answer, and I could only agree. I said, No, probably not, not unless there was a slow, skilled striptease involved, and maybe not even then. She said, Me, either, and I stopped dusting and folded the cloth into a little square and held it in my fist. My feeling then was that I had drunk too much orange juice and the acid was destroying my stomach and maybe the rest of me, too. I sat very still in order to retain my human shape and not release any gases. I looked down at my large thighs, and they reminded me of her husband. She was gathering up her purse and keys. I straightened my back, took a step toward her, and said, I am now going to tell you ten true things about your husband. I held up a finger. Numero uno: he's not a real accountant. She said she already knew this and what were the nine other things. I said there was really only one, the others were just related details. I asked if she had thought of the Indian-restaurant analogy, and she said, What do you mean? I explained it, and she asked if I was making a racist joke, and I said, No, this is a secret true fact. But we were no longer interested in secret true facts, or the truth in any form.

After she left, I stood in the middle of the living room

and decided it was okay to stand there for as long as I wanted. I thought I would eventually get bored, but I did not get bored, I only got worse. I was still holding the dust cloth, and I knew that if I could let it fall, I would be able to move again. But my hand was built to hold this dirty cloth forever. I had been his secretary for three years, and each of these years was made of thousands of moments, all of them unbearable if not for her. This seemed obvious now, that we, or at least I, had labored in her name. As mothers work to feed their children and husbands work for wives. I felt the foundation begin to shake, and in my head I said, Run. But I couldn't run, not from this place that had taken me three years to build. I held the cloth and let everything fall on top of me. My knees buckled, I went down to the floor. I cried in English, I cried in French, I cried in all the languages, because tears are the same all around the world. Esperanto.

I went to work the next day out of curiosity, as people return to their villages after the war to see what is left. The tape dispenser was still standing, and there was my chair and desk, and him and his desk. But everything else was gone. All the invisible things were gone, and in their place, there was just a bad accountant and his secretary. He came over to my desk at noon and said, Ellen tells me you two had a little tête-à-tête. I looked at his sleeve as if it were his face. It had not occurred to me that it would get this bad, that indignity would dance upon bloodshed. I didn't even know what "tête-à-tête" meant. I thought about quitting right then, and also about cutting off all my hair and his hair, too. I thought about cutting off our hair and then mixing it together and lighting it on fire and then quitting. But I did none of these things.

On the last day of class, fruit punch was served, and we all wore our robes. We took them off the machines and ironed them and then put them on over our clothes. We looked like a group of women who know each other very well. Women who wake up together in the morning and stretch and put on their robes. Plaid robes, fuchsia robes, her feather-patterned robe. I stood far away from her, and she stood even farther away from me. I turned to another woman and touched her sash tie and asked how she got the corners so square. She said she had used a pin, that it was easy, that she could show me how. She lifted the ends of my tie into her lap and began picking out the corners. Each pick sent tiny vibrations through the sash and around my waist; I hoped Ellen was watching. There was a softness in the air from all the flannel; it seemed to muffle the chill of the Adult Education Center. Two women were tenderly dabbing at the chest of a third woman who had spilled punch on herself. A group of younger women were braiding each other's hair. But the linoleum between Ellen and me remained measured and waxen. Then Sue suddenly stepped out of the bathroom holding her robe in one hand, naked. She had discovered she couldn't put it on because it wasn't really a robe, it was nothing. All the women paused and fell silent, and Ellen and I quickly looked at each other. Our nakedness was recalled, like a seizure in the air. There was no apology in her eyes, no love or caring. But she saw me, I existed, and this lifted the beams off my shoulders. It takes so little. Sue boldly walked across the room and planted her wad of flannel in the middle of the floor like a pink hive or a giant tulip bulb. All the women gathered around it like fire, like fire we knew better than to touch it, but we could not look away.

The Moves

Before he died, my father taught me his finger moves. They were movements for getting a woman off. He said he didn't know if they'd be of use to me, seeing as how I was a woman myself, but it was all he had in the way of a dowry. I knew what he meant: he meant inheritance, or legacy, not dowry. There were twelve moves in all. He did them on my hand like sign language. They were mostly about speed and pressure in different combinations. There were some flourishes that I never would have thought of. I imagined he'd learned them when he was overseas. A sudden reversal in both speed and direction. Still fingers held like silence for a beat, and then long quick strokes that he called "skinning." I kept wanting to write things down, and he would scoff, asking me if I would take out my notes when the time came. You'll remember, he said, and he repeated skinning on my palm with his dry fingers. It felt like a hand massage. He was incredibly confident. I could not imagine using these movements alone, with such confidence. You're going to make some woman very, very happy, he said. But I knew I had never made anyone very, very happy, and I could only imagine bringing in my dad when the time came to do this. But he would be dead, and I supposed she would be a lesbian and wouldn't want him to touch her. I would have to do the finger moves myself. I would have to decide when she was ready for six and for seven. Could she handle the intensity of the still beat and give in to the rapid pleasures of skinning? I would have to listen to find out. Not just to her breath, my dad said, but to the moisture on the skin in the small of her back. That sweat is your secret emissary. One moment she'll be dry as a cat, and in the next moment—Cape Town is flooding! Don't wait to be sure or you'll miss the boat, hop on and move, move, move.

Each morning when I try to motivate toward something positive, I think of him saying this, and it is a great comfort. I know that one day I'll meet someone special and I'll have a daughter and I'll teach her what he taught me. Don't wait to be sure. Move, move, move.

Mon Plaisir

It's lovely.

I know, but take it off. I want a chin-length bob.

You don't want to go a little bit shorter? What if I cut it to here, to your ears?

You think that'd be better?

No, but then you'd be losing more than ten inches of length, and we could give it to Hair for Care. It's a charity that makes wigs for kids with no hair.

Do you work for them, the charity?

No.

I think I'll just stick with the bob, then.

You could let it grow another inch and then come back and I'll give you a bob. That way everyone wins.

No, I have to do it today. It's the first day of the rest of my life.

Oh. I had a day like that last week.

Really? What happened?

I woke up and thought, This is the first day of the rest of my life.

Then what happened?

I drove to work.

Oh.

Yeah.

Let's give that kid some new hair.

When my husband saw the new short hair, he gave me the look we give each other when one of us forgets who we are. We are not people who buy instant cocoa powder, we do not make small talk, we do not buy Hallmark cards or believe in Hallmark rituals such as Valentine's Day or weddings. In general, we try to stay away from things that are MEANING-LESS, and we favor things that are MEANINGFUL. Our top three favorite meaningful things are: Buddhism, eating right, and the internal landscape. Haircuts are in the same category as trimming the finger- and toenails, which is in the same category as mowing the lawn. We don't really believe in mowing the lawn; we do it only to avoid unnecessary engagement with the neighbors. The neighbors trim their bushes into ridiculous animal shapes. Carl looked at me as if I were the neighbors, as if my hair were in a ridiculous animal shape. Then he continued transcribing a dharma talk by Barry Mendelson, who is sort of a local guru. He does these transcriptions for free for the Zendo we go to. Sometimes the lectures are very long and it takes him over fifty hours to do the transcription. But it is worth it for him, because when the transcribed lecture appears on the Valley Pine Zendo website, he can say: I wrote that, and in a way, this is true.

I went to our bedroom and lay on the floor, so as not to mess up the covers. From where I was lying, I could see dust and old magazines under the bed, and they reminded me of a documentary we had watched about ants. There are entire civilizations under there, just as active as our cities aboveground. We don't have intercourse anymore. I'm not complaining, it's my own fault. I lie there beside him and try to send signals to my vagina, but it's like trying to get cable channels on a TV that doesn't have cable. My mind requests sex, but my vagina is just waiting for the next time it has to pee. It thinks its whole job in life is to pee.

At eight Carl went to tai chi but came home early because the instructor never showed up. A substitute came, but Carl said he was a fake.

You mean he wasn't a real tai chi instructor?

He was a comedian. He kept trying to get everyone to laugh.

Oh. I thought you meant he was an imposter, like a guy off the street.

He also called all the forms by their American names.

Wouldn't that be weird, though, if an actual comedian came in off the street and tried to teach tai chi? Like if Bob Hope tried to teach tai chi?

He called *yun shou* "monkey hands." I'm not paying fourteen dollars a class to do "monkey hands."

We go to bed early and I ask Carl if he wants to nurse, and he does not. Nursing is one of our things. Kind of like Buddhism and eating right, but also kind of not. Actually, the nursing is in a different category. Other things in this category might be:

My unexpressed anger at nothing in particular.

and:

The feeling that there is a "next level" and I should be on it.

Carl would probably have some other things to add to this list that could be called: Important Things That We Don't Understand and Definitely Are Not Going to Talk About. We read in bed for a long time before turning out the light. I read an article about autism. It seems like everywhere you turn these days, there it is, autism. If I had a baby and it started ripping up paper into smaller and smaller bits, it wouldn't take me years to discover the truth. I would instantly think, Holy cow, I've got an autistic, and I would get right to work. But I will not have an autistic child. I won't have a child; I am too old now. Not very too old, just barely. A determined woman might still try, but it is much too late for a woman like me.

I woke at seven A.M. and said to myself: This is the second day of the rest of my life. It's not one thing in particular, it's just the sensation of being adrift. As if the boat became unmoored two days ago and I am now on a voyage. I'm trying to notice everything, like a tourist would, even though it's all familiar. I've done this before; in fact, I was the one who got me and Carl focused on health four years ago. I began with whole-grain bread in our sandwiches, and then came the tai chi, which I never fully got the hang of, and then Buddhism. Carl completely embraced the whole lifestyle after some initial derisive resistance. Sometimes I imagine he was so threatened by my new interests that he joined me out of aggression, as if to say: You can run but you can't hide. I brushed my new short hair with the same long strokes I had used for my old hair, accidentally hitting the brush against my shoulders. It was a delicate, new strangeness, and I held on to it like a candle, hoping it would lead me to an even newer, stranger strangeness. Or perhaps I could accumulate many small new ways and pile them up to form one large new way. With this thought, I drove to the shoe store. I chose a type of shoe that was completely foreign to me. The salesgirl and I stared down at my white veiny feet in their strappy yellow espadrilles.

Do you want me to box those up for you?

No, I'll just wear them out.

I don't recommend that.

Really?

Well, I always wear shoes around the house for a few days first. That way I can still return them if they're uncomfortable.

That's a great tip. Everyone should do that.

People love to make life harder than it has to be.

I know *I* do.

Wear them in the house, that's the first step.

What's the second step?

Wear them outside.

What's the third step?

The third step? You decide.

I wore the new shoes in the car while I drove to therapy, but took them off again before getting out. Every time I enter Ruth's office, dense clouds slide away from my heart to reveal a complex landscape, a gray township, a doomed city. I always become paralyzed in this place, and Ruth has to draw me out with questions, like, What is the worst thing that could happen?

We could never have sex again.

But that's very unlikely.

Well, it feels like I might never want to have it again. Like I wouldn't even care.

I have a client who was in a car accident, and she really *can't* have sex ever again—she's paralyzed. But is their relationship over?

Yes?

No. They have challenges, for sure, but her partner still loves her just as much.

At this point I cry because of the love between this injured woman and her partner, and as I cry, I wonder if

Ruth said "partner" because they are lesbians. Of course they are, and the paralyzed woman is probably running for governor, too. I cry harder. I'd totally vote for her. But does she really exist? Or did Ruth make her up the way I suspect she invents the loving, humorous spats she gets in with her husband. For every argument I have with Carl, Ruth has an anecdote about something similar she went through with her husband—but instead of arguing, he loved her for being a sourpuss, and she laughed sheepishly about what a sourpuss she was. God, it sounds so fucking great; I want to laugh sheepishly at myself, I want to be a sourpuss. Ruth hands me the Kleenex box and our time is up. I half blow my nose, waiting until I get outside to do the full blow.

When I get home, Carl is meditating. I like this time because his eyes are closed; it gives me a chance to be more the way I wish I were around him. I put on the espadrilles and sit on the couch across from his perch on the carpet. First, quietly, I act like a sourpuss, hunching up my shoulders and scowling. Then I sit up and mouth:

Whatsa matter, sourpuss?

I hunch down and mouth: You're always darn meditating.

I sit up: Shucks, sourpuss (somehow the silent versions of me and Carl speak like the Little Rascals), don't go picking on me. I'm workin' on my mind–body duality.

I hunch down sulkily: Meditating, shmeditating. I've got a mind–body duality, too, you know.

I sit up: Of course you do, sourpuss, you're split like a pea.

I hunch down and get ready for my big moment. I squeeze my self tighter, close my mouth, and silently, sheepishly, laugh at myself. Mh, mh, mh, mh. First it is heartbreaking, and I start to cry. But crying is a habit, so I push onward, casting my eyes down under their lids, becoming even more sheepish: Mh, mh, mh, mh. I fall into a rhythm, forgetting laughter, I am just breathing out in intervals of four. With my arms around myself, it is a good feeling, like galloping, mh, mh, mh, mh. As I gallop, I begin to have the sensation that I am galloping alongside Carl, and I wonder if this is meditating. Perhaps I have accidentally fallen into a powerful Indian way of breathing, mh, mh, mh, mh, mh. Maybe it is something that the gurus only teach you after many years' practice. They don't even have it at Carl's Zendo, you have to go to India to learn it, mh, mh, mh, mh. But I stumbled into it the way the Dalai Lamas are innocently born into their positions. I, an ordinary American woman, mh, mh, mh, mh, am doing the ancient forgotten healing breath of India. Won't Carl be jealous when they tell him, when they take me away to a place he can't come to. I'm sorry, I will say, but this is larger than us. He will struggle, he will try to do the ancient breath, mh, mh, mh, mh, and I will laugh, compassionately, because it is such a pathetic imitation, it makes me want to punch him in the face. My breathing is hard and fast, I am shaking my body with tiny vigorous hugs, it is real, the rage is real, it is ancient, it is forgotten, mh, mh, mh, mh! Suddenly, I stop and open my eyes. There is Carl. Feeling my stare, he opens his eyes and looks at me. There I am. Here we are, in the living room.

———

That night he wanted to nurse, so I lifted up my nightgown. I don't have to do anything, my boob is just there, he sucks on it. This always makes me feel sad and thirsty. But they are reversed; the thirst has the depth and tone that sadness should have: thirst as an ache, a howl, a sob. And sadness is pathetically limited to the range of thirst, it is just a sip of emotion, tightly buckled to a frown, quenchable. These feelings probably resolve themselves logically when there is milk in the boob. I could feel Carl's erection against my knee, but I waited it out, and after a while, it went away. He detached from the nipple, and we lay there in the half-darkness I have come to think of as our own.

Have you noticed my new look?

Your haircut?

It's more than that.

Is it internal?

Yes, and I also got new shoes.

Oh.

A car went by outside, and we watched blocks of light slide across the ceiling. Carl pushed down on my foot, and I pressed up on his. This is something we did the first time we ever slept together, it is a seven-year-old gesture. We never really had a proper courtship; we met at a potluck where we quickly discovered that we were both recovering from a break-up. By the time we stopped talking about our exes, we'd been together for a year. I pushed up on Carl's foot, and he pressed down on mine. If the gesture were a person, it'd be in second grade by now. But it is just some movements. Still, I feel closer to him when we do this than at any other time. It is as if our feet are in the perfect, honest, loving relationship, but from the ankles up, we are lost. I push again, but he does not push back; he is asleep.

On the eighth day of the rest of my life, I began to wonder if this was really the rest of my life or just a continuation of the same one. I had so little to go on. Step two was wearing the shoes outside, so I did that. I walked around our neighborhood. I walked onto the busy avenue and right into the popular café the college students like to sit in. I couldn't order anything because I hadn't brought my purse, so I used the bathroom. I used the toilet, the toilet paper, the soap, the water, the paper towels, everything the bathroom had to offer. Then I exited and stared at the community bulletin board. Many of the flyers had a row of rip-off stubs along the bottom; these were also free, so I took one of each. Then I walked home. I lay down on the bedroom floor and looked under the bed and had the exact same set of thoughts about the ant documentary. Whole civilizations. Just like ours. Under there. I flipped onto my stomach and, with my lips against the carpet, I sang the song that goes, "Why must I be a teenager in love?" But without the teenager in love, just "Why must I be?" With the same yearning, though, the same heartache. I took out the paper stubs and laid them out on the carpet. They were all different colors, including Day-Glo. Many of them only had a phone number, with no other points of reference.

I put these mystery stubs in one pile and studied the rest. Three were for missing cats, one was for a free kitten, one was for extras needed for a movie, two were for sublets wanted, one was for a room for rent in a vegan household, and one was for child care wanted. I arranged them according to need, and then in rainbow order. I squinted at the rainbow until it became a pretty blur, and I whispered step three: You decide.

That night I suddenly began missing my hair. I looked up Hair for Care online and scanned the recipient photos. It was definitely too early for it to be a wig on a child's head, but the pictures were still reassuring. The smiling little girls with luxurious hair held photographs of their former, frowning bald selves. I learned that my hair would be combined with nine other ponytails to make a single wig. And my gray hairs would be taken out and sold to a commercial wiggery to offset the costs of postage and website maintenance. So in a sense, I was a busy woman. Parts of me were traveling and offsetting and forming lifelong alliances with parts of other women. I felt uplifted and inspired. I climbed into bed and pushed up on Carl's foot, and he pushed down on mine.

I think we need to move to the next level.

Does that mean children?

You know I'm too old for that.

Just barely, though.

Yeah. But it's not that. It's something I want us to do together.

Is it a sex thing?

No. Why did you say that?

What? I thought you meant, when you said *together,* I thought you—

But you still like our way, don't you?

Can we do it right now?

We did it in our way. Carl nursed and I jacked him off. Then I turned away and touched myself while Carl patted the back of my head. I came, and Carl's hand drifted back to his side of the bed. I turned toward him in the darkness.

Don't go to sleep.

I'm not.

Don't you want to know what the next level is?

What is it?

I'll only tell you if you promise to try it with me.

What if I'm already there?

You're not.

What is it?

You promise you'll do it with me?

Okay.

I think we should become extras. You know, background actors.

As with the whole-grain bread, Carl did not initially leap into the idea with enthusiasm. He laughed when I showed him the neon-green slip of paper with the phone number and the name of the movie: *Hello Maxamillion, Goodbye Maxamillion.* But eventually, he was overwhelmed by my lack of knowledge about the industry. It was so easy to know more than me, Carl could not resist the temptation. And so we began.

———

I was glad to be back in the salon so soon. It was warm and steamy and purred with blow dryers and the smell of professional shampoo. Patrice showed us the thank-you card from Hair for Care, and Carl was impressed. He gave himself to her as if she were taking blood for the Red Cross. Every once in a while I looked up from my magazine to check on his progress. They were little things, a beard trim and haircut, nose and ear hairs trimmed, eyebrows neatened, but I thought they were necessary. If we looked anything other than clean and ordinary, we would pull attention away from the foreground actors.

I couldn't hear what he was saying, but Carl seemed to have opinions; he was in perpetual conversation with Patrice. She would nod, take a step back and look at him as if he were a painting, nod, and begin cutting again. I could have watched this forever, Patrice and Carl talking in the warm, perfumed room. It was not hard to imagine them having sex, her skirt up, him entering her, her hands in his hair as they were. She could suck him; he would like that. I felt kindly toward Carl and like a sister to Patrice. "Sister" was too strong a word, really; I wanted her to beg for it. I bequeathed all kinds of desperation to her; I gave her things I wasn't sure I even had. She leaned in, carefully trimming his eyebrows, and then stepped back, twirled him around, and asked, What do you think?

———

159

I suggested we go to the shoe store next, but Carl pointed out that you rarely saw the shoes of people in movies.

But that's because they go close up on their faces. They won't be close on our faces; we'll be walking around in the background with our shoes showing.

If we're far away enough for our shoes to be showing, then we're too far away for anyone to see them clearly.

I thought about this, and it seemed true. It was strange how Carl seemed to know things about cinematography and the trade. When he was initially ridiculing my idea, he scoffed and said, Even if it wasn't a silly, low-level, almost offensively banal idea, we still couldn't do it because we aren't in the guild.

What guild?

The union of background actors.

Is there really such a thing?

Well, you don't think they'd just let anyone waltz onto a set, do you?

But they do; later, we looked it up on instantcast.com and found out that many movies hire regular people after they fulfill their union quotas. We also read about how important extras are; they aren't "extra" at all. Imagine a busy saloon in the old west. *When the bad guy walks in, how do we know he's bad? Because hundreds of background actors freeze in midaction, beer glasses raised halfway to lips, cards half shuffled, darts frozen in midair.* I read this aloud to Carl after he finished his nightly dharma talk transcription.

Now can I read something to you?

What?

Yes or no.

Yes.

When you can see the beauty of a tree, then you will know what love is.

That's beautiful.

I think it is.

Did you just transcribe that?

Yeah, it came to me after dinner.

Came to you . . . through the headphones.

Right.

On the third day of the rest of Carl's life, and the eleventh day of mine, I began calling the number. Instantcast.com explained that your willingness to hit redial for hours at a time *is* the screening process. This is the actual, professional way that one applies for this job, in the manner of a person trying to win tickets off the radio. The directors are looking for people who are willing to do almost anything, but will happily do almost nothing, for hours.

While I pressed redial, I visited many websites about background acting, and these sites were linked to sites about famous Hollywood stars, and these sites were linked to sites about adult movie stars, and eventually, I found myself watching the personal webcam of a pretty young woman named Savannah Banks. Savannah wasn't naked, like I would've thought. She was at her desk, first doing something that looked like paying bills, and then making phone calls. It looked as though she was checking her messages, but after a while, I realized she might be pressing redial, like me. I was suddenly sure she was on hold for the *Hello Maxamillion, Good-bye Maxamillion* casting call. If they took her call first, I was going to be very frustrated. She didn't need this like I did; she lived alone, she had a webcam, she had many, many options. She leaned back in her chair, waiting. I could wait, too. We were locked in a dead heat, a stalemate. And then, I won.

Casting.

Hello! I'm calling about the casting call?

Which one?

Hello Maxamillion, Goodbye Maxamillion?

Oh, that's been cast.

Really?

Yes.

Oh.

Yeah. Well, then.

Well.

Okay, maybe they still need one more person. I don't know for sure, but they might still need one more person if you go down there right now.

Oh, but it's not just me, it's my husband, too, and he's at tai chi right now.

Well, two is unlikely.

But that's the whole point—this is for us together.

I don't know, maybe they need two, I really don't know. You think?

You guys should just go down there.

Really?

What have you got to lose?

Nothing.

Bring three shirts each.

I'll bring four!

I hung up and looked once more at Savannah. She was putting on her coat and grabbing her purse. I gathered up our shirts and stood in the driveway. She had an unfair advantage because I had to wait for Carl.

It was a tragic romance. Maxamillion was an old man who falls in love with a child and waits for her to grow up, only to die of old age on her eighteenth birthday. We were in an early scene, where Maxamillion takes his six-year-old love interest to a fancy French restaurant called Mon Plaisir. We and twenty-two other extras were paired and clustered at tables with long tablecloths. Maxamillion and the girl were right beside us, holding hands and looking into each other's eyes in a way that I, for one, felt uncomfortable with. But it was not my place to judge the love between these two fictional characters. Dave, the assistant director, told us to talk and eat just as we normally would if we were enjoying a meal at a fancy French restaurant, but to take tiny bites, so the meals would last for the next four to five hours. Carl looked down at his plate; not eating French food was easy for us, because we're macrobiotic. And action!

Hi.

Hi, Carl.

We don't normally say hi at dinner.

I'm going to drink some of my water now.

Me, too.

No, we can't both drink water!

Why not?

That's not real.

But I'm really thirsty.

Well, just wait.

Carl leaned back in his chair, waiting.

What are you doing? We have to keep talking!

Well, clearly I'm not an actor, but then it wasn't my idea, was it?

Oh, terrific, so now it's my fault for—

CUT! Cut, cut, cut, cut!

Wherein we learned our first big lesson about background acting. When Dave told us to talk as we normally would at a fancy French restaurant, he meant talk as you normally would but *don't use sound*. Talk silently. He thought we knew. No. We didn't even know why we were here. Where was Savannah Banks? I glanced around, but she wasn't at Mon Plaisir. Of course she wasn't. She probably didn't even live in this city. She was probably on a real date at a real French restaurant. I looked at Carl and he looked at me. Our bleak reality was now apparent: we couldn't leave and we couldn't change partners. Maxamillion stroked the little girl's hand with a wrinkled finger, and Dave called action.

Suddenly we were actors. We alternated like people talking, we listened and nodded and laughed silently and ate tiny bites of food. We moved our mouths and faces, we gestured occasionally to emphasize, we animated ourselves as young couples animate themselves when they are talking. Carl even interrupted me, mouthing and nodding in agreement with what I was saying, presumably taking it one step further, and I just knew, knowing the way that people talk when they are happy, that he had said something funny. I laughed soundlessly and Carl smiled, a real smile, so pleased was he to have made me laugh. And it was so tremendous to see that smile, I could feel myself glowing, I somehow felt beautiful, and cut.

We said nothing now that we were allowed to speak. We couldn't even look at each other; it was too embarrassing. I waited nervously for action, and when Dave yelled out, I looked up, meeting Carl's eyes as they crinkled into a smile. How striking he was in his collared shirt with his new haircut. He poured more wine, and we raised our glasses and mouthed, To us! And by "us" I knew we both meant not *us* but these two people who had met for the first time at Mon Plaisir. I slid my hand across the table, Carl quickly covered it in his, I bloomed like a struck match. And cut.

Again we waited with our eyes lowered. His hand remained on mine, but lifelessly, and as lights were adjusted around us, I had time to wonder how many more takes were left. There could not be enough.

On action, I squeezed Carl's finger and he gripped mine. The urgency seemed obvious now, we both leaned forward and I held his bearded chin as we kissed quickly, not wanting to distract from the lead table. The feeling between us was mournful and desperate. We could not look away from each other, every inhalation was a question: Yes? Followed by: Yes. Falling and catching and falling and catching, we descended into a precarious and vivid place; I had always known it was there but had never guessed where. Carl's new sense of humor flourished in silence, he made subtly absurd gestures that surprised me into almost audible laughter. And I could not make a move without making love. Every time I shifted in my chair, lifted my fork, brushed my hair from my eyes, I seemed to be pushing through the motions as through honey, slowly and with all kinds of implications. I feared our breath was too loud. I seized his forearms, he took off his shoes, beneath the table, our feet pushed with an almost vocal eloquence. Dave cried, Cut, and then:

That's a wrap for our background, thank you, background actors!

How could it be over? Carl and I looked at each other with disbelief. The crew began to clap, everyone clapped; we could only rise from our table and stumble out of the room with the twenty-two other diners. We didn't look at each other when we parted toward different dressing rooms. The drive home was long and sealed in a drowning silence. Walking across the front lawn, Carl stopped to re-coil the hose that I had left out the day before. I waited for him for a moment and then felt silly standing there and went inside. It was late, so I started making dinner. Only once we sat down did it strike me as bizarre. Here we were again, eating together in silence. I pressed my fork into the greens and began to cry. Carl looked up, we stared across the table at each other. It was plain between us: we should not be together any longer. And cut.

In the weeks that followed, we amazed ourselves. Our habits slid apart easily; I woke up early in the guest room; he stayed up late chatting with Buddhist strangers on the Internet. Like college roommates, we instinctively used different shelves in the refrigerator for the foods we now bought separately. It turned out we didn't really like to eat the same things. We searched for new places to live, sometimes seizing on the same apartment listing. And our very few intimacies were simply discontinued. Where did they go, those things we did? Were they recycled? Did some new couple in China do them? Were a Swedish man and woman foot to foot at this very moment? We helped each other move, first loading boxes into a studio he had found in our neighborhood, then driving the U-Haul across town to my new place. When the truck was empty, we hugged and I thought: In less than one minute, I will be walking into my new home. Carl gave me a salute through the window and drove away. I turned and walked toward my new front door. This is it, I thought. Here I go. But before I reached the door I heard a honk. He was back. I had left a trowel in the front seat. We discussed what to do with it; neither of us had a yard now. I began to feel that the conversation about the trowel might never end. I saw us as two old people standing on the sidewalk with the trowel between us. I quickly took the tool from Carl and held it against my chest. He got back in the car and I walked toward the door with the trowel in hand. This is it, I thought. I'm alone now. I looked down the street to be sure. Yes.

Birthmark

On a scale of one to ten, with ten being childbirth, this will
be a three.

A three? Really?

Yes. That's what they say.

What other things are a three?

Well, five is supposed to be having your jaw reset.

So it's not as bad as that.

No.

What's two?

Having your foot run over by a car.

Wow, so it's worse than that?

But it's over quickly.

Okay, well, I'm ready. No—wait; let me adjust my sweater. Okay, I'm ready.

All right, then.

Here goes a three.

The laser, which had been described as pure white light, was more like a fist slammed against a countertop, and her body was a cup on the counter, jumping with each slam. It turned out three was just a number. It didn't describe the pain any more than money describes the thing it buys. Two thousand dollars for a port-wine stain removed. A kind of birthmark that seems messy and accidental, as if this red area covering one whole cheek were the careless result of too much fun. She spoke to her body like an animal at the vet, Shhh, it's okay, I'm sorry, I'm so sorry we have to do this to you. This is not unusual; most people feel that their bodies are innocent of their crimes, like animals or plants. Not that this was a crime. She had waited patiently from the time she was fourteen for aesthetic surgery to get cheap, like computers. Nineteen ninety-eight was the year lasers came to the people as good bread, eat and be full, be finally perfect. Oh yes, perfect. She didn't think she would have bothered if she hadn't been what people call "very beautiful except for." This is a special group of citizens living under special laws. Nobody knows what to do with them. We mostly want to stare at them like the optical illusion of a vase made out of the silhouette of two people kissing. Now it is a vase . . . now it could only be two people kissing . . . oh, but it is so completely a vase. It is both! Can the world sustain such a contradiction? And this was even better, because as the illusion of prettiness and horribleness flipped back and forth, we flipped with it. We were uglier than her, then suddenly we were lucky not to be her, but then again, at this angle she was too lovely to bear. She was both, we were both, and the world continued to spin.

Now began the part of her life where she was just very beautiful, except for nothing. Only winners will know what this feels like. Have you ever wanted something very badly and then gotten it? Then you know that winning is many things, but it is never the thing you thought it would be. Poor people who win the lottery do not become rich people. They become poor people who won the lottery. She was a very beautiful person who was missing something very ugly. Her winnings were the absence of something, and this quality hung around her. There was so much potential in the imagined removal of the birthmark; any fool on the bus could play the game of guessing how perfect she would look without it. Now there was not this game to play, there was just a spent feeling. And she was no idiot, she could sense it. In the first few months after the surgery, she received many compliments, but they were always coupled with a kind of disorientation.

Now you can wear your hair up and show off your face more.

Yeah, I'm going to try it that way.

Wait, say that again.

"I'm going to try it that way." What?

Your little accent is gone.

What accent?

You know, the little Norwegian thing.

Norwegian?

Isn't your mom Norwegian?

She's from Denver.

But you have that little bit of an accent, that little ... way of saying things.

I do?

Well, not anymore, it's gone now.

And she felt a real sense of loss. Even though she knew she had never had an accent. It was the birthmark, which in its density had lent color even to her voice. She didn't miss the birthmark, but she missed her Norwegian heritage, like learning of new relatives, only to discover they have just died.

All in all, though, this was minor, less disruptive than insomnia (but more severe than déjà vu). Over time she knew more and more people who had never seen her with the birthmark. These people didn't feel any haunting absence, why should they? Her husband was one of these people. You could tell by looking at him. Not that he wouldn't have married a woman with a port-wine stain. But he probably wouldn't have. Most people don't and are none the worse for it. Of course, sometimes it would happen that she would see a couple and one of them would have a port-wine stain and the other would clearly be in love with this stained person and she would hate her husband a little. And he could feel it.

Are you being weird?

No.

You are.

Actually, I'm not. I'm just eating my salad.

I can see them, too, you know. I saw them come in.

Hers is worse than mine was. Mine didn't go down on my neck like that.

Do you want to try this soup?

I bet he's an environmentalist. Doesn't he look like one?

Maybe you should go sit with them.

Maybe I will.

I don't see you moving.

Did you just finish the soup? I thought we were splitting.

I offered it to you.

Well, you can't have any of this salad, then.

It was a small thing, but it was a thing, and things have a way of either dying or growing, and it wasn't dying. Years went by. This thing grew, like a child, microscopically, every day. And since they were a team, and all teams want to win, they continuously adjusted their vision to keep its growth invisible. They wordlessly excused each other for not loving each other as much as they had planned to. There were empty rooms in the house where they had meant to put their love, and they worked together to fill these rooms with midcentury modern furniture. Herman Miller, George Nelson, Charles and Ray Eames. They were never alone; it became crowded. The next sudden move would have to be through the wall. What happened was this. She was trying to get the lid off a new jar of jam, and she was banging it on the counter. This is a well-known tip, a kitchen trick, a bang to loosen the lid. It's not witchery or black magic, it's simply a way to release the pressure under the lid. She banged it too hard, and the jar broke. She screamed. Her husband came running when he heard the sound. There was red everywhere, and in that instant he saw blood. Hallucinatory clarity: you are certain of what you see. But in the next moment, your fear relinquishes control: it was jam. Everywhere. She was laughing, picking shards of glass out of the strawberry mash. She was laughing at the mess, and her face was down, looking at the floor, and her hair was around her face like a curtain, and then she looked up at him and said, Can you bring the trash can over here?

And it happened again. For a moment he thought he saw a port-wine stain on her cheek. It was fiercely red and bigger than he had ever imagined. It was bloodier than even blood, like sick blood, animal blood, the blood racist people think beats inside people of other races: blood that shouldn't touch my own. But the next moment it was just jam, and he laughed and rubbed the kitchen towel on her cheek. Her clean cheek. Her port-wine stain.

Honey.

Can you get the trash can?

Honey.

What?

Go look in the mirror.

What?

Go look in the mirror.

Stop talking like that. Why are you talking like that? What?

He was looking at her cheek. She instinctively put her hand on the mark and ran to the bathroom.

She was in there for a long time. Maybe thirty minutes. You've never had thirty minutes like these. She stared at the port-wine stain and she breathed in and she breathed out. It was like being twenty-three again, but she was thirty-eight now. Fifteen years without it, and now here it was. In the same exact place. She rubbed her finger around its edges. It came as high as her right eye, over to the edge of her right nostril, across her whole cheek to the ear, ending at her jawbone. In purplish-red. She wasn't thinking anything, she wasn't afraid or disappointed or worried. She was looking at the stain the way one would look at oneself fifteen years after one's own death. Oh, you again. Now it was obvious it had always been there; she had startled it back into sight. She looked into its redness and breathed in and breathed out and found herself in a kind of trance. She thought: I am in a kind of trance. She was just blowing around. It lasted about twenty-five minutes, a very, very long time to be just blowing around. Mostly, you waft for a second or two, a half second, maybe. And then you spend the rest of your life trying to describe it, to regain the perspective. You say, It was like I was just blowing around, and you wave your arms in the air. But there were no arms like that, and you know it. She came out of the trance like a plane taking off. Instead of being inside the stain, she was now looking down on it from above. Like a lake, it grew smaller and smaller until it was only a tiny region in a larger mass. One that this pilot favored, hovered over, but would not touch down on again. She pulled some toilet paper off the roll and blew her nose.

He found himself kneeling. He was waiting for her on his knees. He was worried she would not let him love her with the stain. He had already decided long ago, twenty or thirty minutes ago, that the stain was fine. He had only seen it for a moment, but he was already used to it. It was good. It somehow allowed them to have more. They could have a child now, he thought. There was a loose feeling in the air. The jam was still on the floor, and that was okay. He would just kneel here and wait for her to come out and hope he would be able to tell her about the looseness in a loose way. He wanted to keep the feeling. He hoped she wasn't removing it somehow, the stain. She should keep it, and they should have a kid. He could hear her blowing her nose; now she was opening the door. He would stay on his knees, just like this. She would see him this way and understand.

How to Tell Stories to Children

Tom had done some bad things. Now, it seemed, he was getting his comeuppance. There was almost nothing to say that the universe had not said already. I asked about his wife.

Is Sarah willing to talk about it?

Sure, but she's blasé. She doesn't give a shit.

That's terrible.

Yeah.

And the student?

She won't stop fucking him.

Oh man. Man oh man.

Yeah.

And she knows about your, your things—your affairs?

No.

We sat in silence, sipping our tea. And to think that twelve years ago I had been one of these things. I pressed my finger against a cold tea bag. A few minutes later, we embraced and went our separate ways.

He didn't call me for a few weeks. This was customary within our friendship, confide and retreat, but I wondered. I wondered if perhaps our last conversation had been an overture. Not the conversation, exactly, but the silences within it. There had been many dark pits of tea-sipping silence; looking back, I could imagine placing my hand on his hand while kneeling in one of these dark pits. And in such a pit could one even be sure what one was doing? One might seek solace in a friend and literally go inside this friend to get the solace; and the friend, being old and familiar, might give especially good solace. With this kindness in mind, I e-mailed Tom.

Lunch?

And he responded:

Sarah is pregnant and we're having the baby!! More soon, I have to run. Just wanted you to hear it from me first. Love, Tom

At the baby shower, Tom's mother walked around with a clipboard assigning all the guests days on which to bring a healthy meal to the new parents. It was called a meal tree, like a telephone tree. If Tom and Sarah did not answer the door,

I was told, I should leave the meal on the front porch in a basket that would be labeled: *Thank You Friends!*

Luckily, I was allocated the last possible day, and I hoped that the passing of time would carry me out of horror toward feelings of joy. But the day came and I had no such feelings. I knocked on their door very quietly, hoping to leave the meal in the *Thank You Friends* basket, which actually said *Put Meals Here*. The door swung open immediately.

Deb, thank God you're here, can you take her?

And the baby was handed to me. Tom guided us past a tear-stained Sarah, who gave a sarcastic wave, and into the office/baby room. Tom looked at me and winced apologetically before shutting the door and leaving us alone. There was a silence, and then,

I didn't say that! I said I could have if I wanted to because it's my body!

But our baby was in your body! You could have hurt her!

It's perfectly safe as long as it's not rough sex!

Oh. So it did happen.

I held my breath and pulled the child to my chest as if she were me. There was a long silence during which I imagined Sarah weeping silently. But suddenly, her voice issued, clear and unadorned with guilt.

Yeah.

Yeah. And what was this not-rough sex like if it was not rough?

It was gentle.

They were in a wilderness that was too wild for me, they were living with bears, they were bears, their words flew past deadly animal teeth. I wished I were hearing about this in second or even third hand: "We had a terrible fight," "I heard they had a terrible fight," "I had an acquaintance who knew a couple who, back in the early part of the century, had a terrible fight, perhaps even had terrible fights on a regular basis, this acquaintance doesn't know for sure, she is realizing now that she didn't really know the couple, on account of the fact that she had mixed intentions with regard to the man in the couple, intentions that now are even more ancient history than this ancient, historical, terrible fight."

Tom began screaming, and I wondered if the baby's soft brain was, in this moment, changing shape in response to the violent stimuli. I tried to intellectualize the noise to protect the baby's psyche. I whispered: Isn't that interesting to hear a man scream? Doesn't that challenge our stereotypes of what men can do? And then I tried, Shhhhhhhhh.

She burrowed for a nipple, and I slipped my finger into her mouth. As she slept in my arms, I found I could only think thoughts that were cosmological in scale. I considered the round ball of the sun, the food cycle, and time itself, which seemed miraculous and poignant. I curled my whole body around her. Tom and Sarah were distant traffic beside my primeval blossoming, the almost painful expansion of my heart to include their descendent. I studied each scale model of a finger; I gazed at her shut eyes with their majestic lashes, and her good intention of a nose. But I could not remember her name. I looked at her face. Lilya? No, it was something less innocent, more overly clever. I stared at a stuffed bunny and a row of acrobatic wooden clowns on a shelf. Lana? No. The clowns leaned and bent and gradually came into focus. They were not only acrobatic, they were alphabetic, and they would contort forever to spell the name Lyon.

Throughout time there have been women who came by their children gradually, organically, without the formalities of conception or adoption. It felt intuitive to me but was a confusing situation for my boyfriends.

Didn't we just see Lyon?

Not since she learned to swim with water wings.

But can one really call that swimming?

Oh, come on, you know how afraid she is of water. It's a big, huge deal.

How about "it's a big deal" and we save "big, huge deal" for us? Can we do that? Can we save that for something big and huge that happens to us?

Like what?

Like, I don't know, a big, huge . . . feeling between us.

Uh-oh, this sounds like it's about to be a long conversation. Look, you don't have to go. Just drop me off and pick me up at four.

She is running toward me, covered in hundreds of water droplets, a pink-and-yellow-flowered swimsuit, sunlight in her eyes, red mouth broken open into a shout, crashing wetly into my legs with so much to say.

I went in before but that was holding on to the side and then today this morning I went in again, holding on to the side, but then I let go! I let go! And I couldn't touch the bottom! And it was for nine seconds! But I think I can do it longer but I had to rest on a towel because I was so tired and Daddy said you were coming over so I waited, I've been waiting for almost a million years, can we go in now? Did you see my towel? See, it has a picture of a teenager with a bikini and a little dog, don't step on it, you messed it up, can you fix it, please? Yeah. Can we go in now? Can you hold me at first?

We bobbed around in the middle of the pool, her legs wrapped around my waist, one arm around my neck, the other directing us through the water. We were heavy and clumsy but also weightless and graceful. In the deep end, she gripped me and screamed; in the shallow end, she broke free and marveled at her own bravery. She checked the water wings every couple of minutes, pressing on them to make sure they were still hard.

I think this one's going down.

No, it's fine.

Can you blow it up a little more?

I don't want to pop it.

Can you check it?

It's fine, see? It's the same as the other one.

She felt the other one, looked up at me solemnly, opened her eyes wide, and then jumped up and down, shouting, splashing, reckless. Sarah looked up from her magazine and then looked down again. Tom looked across the patio, our eyes met, and for a split second I remembered my drunken nineteen-year-old face pressed against his chest at a party, his lips resting on the top of my head, murmuring, You know I wish I could. It seemed impossible that I ever thought of him as the main attraction. Now he was Lyon's father, and she possessed the daring, the warmth, the wicked charm I once thought I would find in him. Lyon plunged her face into the water and held a winged arm in the air; her fist released a spiky finger for each second endured. One, two, three, four, five, the other arm shot up, six, seven, eight, nine, ten—her arms froze in the air, all digits holding numbers—and then her face, smeared with wet hair and mucus, rose out of the depths. Gasping, furious, she shook her stiff hands at me.

I ran out of fingers! That was longer than ten seconds! You saw it was longer! Did you count?

I think it was thirteen.

I think it might have been twenty-seven!

Do you want to know how to count higher? You just start over on the first hand.

No.

You remember ten, and you start on the first hand with eleven.

I said no. I don't want to know.

But how will you count big numbers?

When it goes bigger than ten, you can do it.

Okay, but what if I'm not there?

At this she laughed. She jumped out of the pool and ran toward her mother on the lounger. She shrieked, now in a drunken imitation of laughter, and hurled herself onto Sarah.

What's so funny?

Deb.

She is funny, isn't she. A funny bunny.

Friday night was date night, named for the date Sarah and Tom would go on while Lyon slept over at my house. But because they usually just stayed home and fought, and Lyon and I more often went to dinner and saw a movie, date night became our code for Night of Endless Fun. Don't under-estimate how much joy an eight-year-old and an almost-forty-year-old can bring each other. We usually began at Miso Happy, our favorite Japanese place. We thought the name was terrible, but we liked the noodles. We talked about every-thing, including but not limited to: My gray hairs, should I dye them? Could I dye them individually? Could I pay a mouse with a tiny paintbrush to jump on my head and dye them one by one? And why did Tom and Sarah have to fight so much? Was it Lyon's fault? No, absolutely not. Could she stop them from fighting? Again, no. Also: would they buy her a twenty-four-color pen set, and, if they did, how jealous would best friend Claire be when Lyon brought it to school? Our guess was very. And why had Deb's last boyfriend dumped her?

I dumped *him*.

Maybe you didn't French-kiss him enough.

I promise you that wasn't it.

Tell me how many times a day you kissed, and I'll say if it was enough.

Four hundred.
Not enough.

If there was a decent kid movie, we would see that after dinner, but usually, we went to the second-run theater, where
we saw things like *McCabe & Mrs. Miller* or *Bonnie and Clyde*
or *Shampoo*. We were massive Warren Beatty fans. I worried
at first about the sex and violence, but Lyon discovered that
as long as the movie was made before 1986, she could take
it. Thus, *Reds* was okay, but *Ishtar* was too disturbing. After
the movie, we came home and took a bath in my tub, also
known as La Salon Paree. We made potions out of combinations of shampoos and tested them on each other's backs
for scent, froth, and beautification properties. We checked
Lyon's body for signs of puberty, which never appeared. (Or
yes, they did, but years after the close of La Salon Paree.)
We slept together in my giant bed that was exactly as wide
as it was long. It made as much sense to sleep in one direction as another, and Lyon charted our course by spinning
around, Tonight weee willlll sleeeeeep, and then flinging
herself down, this way! She lay still, holding the spot, while
I moved the pillows around to our new north. We read from
an antique book called *How to Tell Stories to Children, and
Some Stories to Tell*. Lyon was bored by the prosaic "Billy Beg
and His Ball" and "The Fox and the Ox," but she loved to
hear me read the chapter called "The Storyteller's Mood—
A Few Principles of Method, Manner, and Voice, from the
Psychological Point of View." And then we slept. Spooning

at first, and then, because Lyon radiated an uncomfortable heat, back to back.

By the time she was nine, she was living at my house three or four days a week, and Sarah and Tom were sleeping at other people's houses most of the time. Sometimes Tom, in a moment of manic elation, would suggest I meet his current girlfriend.

It's only because she's gorgeous, and I think you would appreciate that.

Well, thank you, but that's okay.

Oh. Are you jealous?

No.

But you would have been when we were younger.

Probably.

Sarah sure is. Do you at least want to see a picture?

No.

What do you think of her? Is she not perfect?

She is.

Do you want to keep the picture?

What would I do with it?

I don't know, you could put it on your refrigerator.

I wouldn't want Lyon to see it.

Oh, she's already met her.

When Lyon was ten, she entered a spiritual phase. None of us three was religious, so she drew from a wide array of sources. She called it the Pleiades, an ever-evolving combination of mythology, Anne Frank, and gleanings from her friend Claire, who went to Sunday school and wore a crucifix. She could add and subtract rituals as they were needed;

some days were Days of Darkness, and she asked me to either cover my face with a veil or just stay away from her. On Ms. Frank's birthday, we cried, and those of us who could not spontaneously cry were given the option of whispering every bad thing we had ever done to the last page of the book, the page before they are discovered by the SS. The Pleiades derived much of its authority from an ability to conjure guilt. Lyon wore my castoff silver Gaia pendant, which was abstractly vaginal in a way she wasn't aware of, and pretended to loathe wearing it. When Claire made a big fuss about having to wear her stupid old cross, Lyon said, Tell me about it, my parents make me wear this.

What is that?

It's for our religion.

Are you Jewish?

No, it's really complicated. Here, let me show you, take off your shirt.

What are you gonna do?

Just touch your back with my necklace.

Oh, that. That's not religious. My mom does it with her nails, we call it Backles.

Backles?

Yeah.

She touches your back like this?

Yeah.

No offense, but your mom might be a pervert.

No she's not.

Backles is actually called foreplay, and it's to get you in the mood.

What mood?

Reckless abandon.

That night in bed Lyon handed me the Gaia pendant. Backles was never directly affiliated with the Pleiades, but I performed it religiously for months, dangling the necklace first from one hand and then, when that got tired, from the other.

The Pleiades had real staying power; at age twelve, Lyon was still of the faith. She had forsaken the pendant and the more familiar rituals for a series of mystical practices, as Jews sometimes pursue the kabbalah. One night she carefully ripped three flowery sheets into wide strips and asked me to swaddle her like a mummy in celebration of the Day of Hooray, which was like the Pleiades Christmas.

Tighter.

I think that's as tight as it can be.

Okay. Thank you.

She lay armless and inert, staring at the ceiling.

What if you have to go to the bathroom?

I'll go in here.

Okay.

All right. Good night, Deb.

Good night. Happy Hooray Day. Hooray!

Hooray.

In the middle of the night, I was woken by her yelling, which might have been expected, I mean my God, how uncomfortable. I unwound the pee-soaked strips while she sobbed to the point of coughing.

I thought I was going to die.

Well, I never should have let you do it.

Don't say that!

But look at you, honey, you're freezing, you're upset and crying.

That's the ceremony! That's the end part of the ceremony!

Okay, well, great. Hooray.

Hooray! I'm okay!

In the fall of 2001, I met a man named Ed Borger. We all did, actually, the four of us met with Ed Borger once a week; he was our family counselor. This was the year when Lyon had acute allergies, a rageful year spent entirely in my care. The counseling was Tom's idea; I think he hoped this professional outsider would be stunned by our mess and blame Sarah, the mother, for it. But Ed wasn't fazed; in fact, he suggested the dynamic had served each of us well. Something in the way he said this gave me the feeling that the dynamic was moving on, perhaps down the block, where it would serve some other confused family. And we would be left dynamic-less, four people alone with all the wrong feelings for one another.

The first few sessions were familiar to Lyon and me: we watched while Tom and Sarah slaughtered each other and then rose from the dead to love each other and then became bored. Lyon rolled her eyes at me and even attempted to mouth, Let's get frozen yogurt after, okay? which I ignored for Ed Borger's sake. Ed was, in my honest opinion, a wonderful man. I was paying my one third of the $150, and I wanted to be transformed by him. In time, Lyon and I were encouraged to talk more. Lyon gave a gorgeously self-centered speech in which she enumerated her emotional needs.

I need peace and quiet and no fighting when I'm doing my homework and sleeping. I need a black JanSport backpack—

Hon, that's not really an emotional need—

I need Mommy to shut up and let me finish my list because who is she to say if it's an emotional need or not. I need to stay at Deb's house when I feel like it.

Here Ed gently pressed her.

Do you prefer living at Deborah's house?

Yeah, but my mom doesn't like it.

(Mom opens her mouth and then shuts it.)

Why do you think she doesn't like it?

Because, you know, Deb and my dad.

(My left hand grips my right; Tom looks at the floor.)

What about Deb and your dad?

You know.

No, I don't. Do you feel comfortable saying what you are thinking?

They used to be married. That's why Deb's, like, my other mom.

(Tom gasps, Sarah laughs, I speak.)

We were never married, we're just friends! We've always been friends.

Oh. But what about—

What?

190

Oh, I don't know. I thought . . . I don't know. Well, thanks for telling me, everyone. Now I feel dumb.

And we all rushed in at once to tell the child that she was not dumb, she was the opposite of dumb, she was insightful and sensitive and possibly even clairvoyant. Perhaps she was remembering something from a past lifetime? We laughed; maybe she knew something we didn't! Maybe that's why we were such good friends in this lifetime! Ed Borger observed us from a kind distance, clearly not buying any of it but not judging, just watching the dynamic serve us another round, just one more round, please.

I was premenstrual on the day Ed Borger finally forced me to speak. But I did not speak. Instead, I wept at various different pitches and velocities, using my wail to describe a devastating unhappiness that surprised us all. After the session, my three people hugged me, and within their tangle, I felt safe. Lyon held my hand, and Tom asked if I wanted to talk about my feelings. I looked at him and his child, and for a fraction of a second, I could see the spell that bound me, like a spider thread catching the light. Cast upon me long ago, at an age when I longed to be ensnared, it now spanned generations. Sarah rubbed my back with a chilly palm, the vision disappeared, and I felt certain I had nothing to say.

We had seen Ed for a whole month, nearly five sessions, and we all felt he had helped us a lot and we were ready to stop family counseling. Some of us (Sarah) had been ready to stop since before we started, but now we had consensus; Lyon's acute allergies had gone away.

When Lyon's eyes and skin did become red and inflamed, Sarah was prone to saying things like, Is this your way of seeking attention? Allergies? That's the best you can do? Ed taught Lyon to say, Mom, I need you to take care of me, and he taught Sarah to respond without yelling. They had tried the technique in my living room; Lyon said her line perfectly, and Sarah had mastered the gentle tone but veered somewhat off course, whispering, Tell me how I can help my little girl, my big little girl, do you really want me to talk like this? Doesn't this make you feel like a baby?

Thus it may have been in self-defense that Lyon's aggravated preteen body replaced itself with an unaggravated, rather amazing woman's body in the summer after her freshman year of high school. I thought this elegantly bubble-bottomed response was brilliant; I could not have said it better myself.

Ed had also suggested we work our way back to joint custody, so Lyon begrudgingly began to sleep at home two nights a week. It was hard to know what to do with myself on these evenings. I wasn't used to sleeping alone, though I'd long since stopped having boyfriends. The first night I usually spent cleaning, but the second sent me into a spin. After a while I learned to clean more slowly, spreading it out over two fairly pleasant nights, which were always punctuated by a call from Lyon.

Mom is out with Juan, and Dad is in the garage talking on his cell phone.

What are you doing?

I don't know, I might call Kevin and ask him to come over here and lick me.

Lyon.

What? I talked to him today.

No, you did not.

Yeah, in seminar.

What happened?

He said—

He initiated? That's good.

I know.

Okay, go.

He said, I bet you've already read the whole book—

—*My Ántonia*?

Yeah. And I said, No I haven't even finished last night's pages. And that's all.

That's good. He thinks you're smart.

I know. I'm going to masturbate thinking about him now.

Okay, you do that.

I'm kidding! Like I would tell you if I was going to.

By the time I ran into Ed Borger at Trader Joe's, Lyon was living at my house only half the week. Which is something Ed and I talked about with loaves of bread in our hands. He thought this was great progress. I said we owed it all to him. He said his bread always got moldy before he could finish the loaf. I said he should freeze the bread to prevent this problem. He said, Won't that ruin the bread? I said, Not if you're making toast with it. He said, You can just toast it frozen? And I said, Yep.

We put our groceries in our respective cars and guessed

that we had about forty minutes before our perishables perished, enough time for a cup of tea.

Back when we were in family counseling, I used to daydream, what if Ed only wanted to hear what *I* thought, what if the rest of the family weren't even allowed in the room, what if I could just talk and talk and talk and what if when I was done Ed told me I was a genius and the rest of the bunch were loony tunes and then what if Ed said he had always been attracted to me and what if he took off my clothes and I took off his clothes and we held each other for more or less the rest of our lives. I will admit this thought was in the back of my mind while we sipped our tea. Mostly, we talked about Lyon.

I think she's going to become a terrific woman one day.

She almost already is! She's grown a lot since you last saw her.

She's taller?

Yeah. And she's more developed.

Developed.

Yeah. Which seems to have calmed her allergies. Do you think that's possible? Medically speaking?

Well, anything's possible, medically speaking.

I feel the same way.

What do you mean?

That anything's possible.

Well, not anything. Pigs can't fly.

Yeah, but for some reason, sitting here with you, I feel like they can.

Can?

Fly.

Oh.

I'm sorry, am I being ridiculous?

No, no, you're not, no.

Ed Borger put his yogurt in my refrigerator and asked me to remind him to get it before he left. Lyon was at her parents' house, but her clothes were all over the bed. I picked them off and put them on the dresser. I turned out the light, and we did not take off each other's clothes, but we each took off our own clothes. Before we did anything, Ed asked if he had permission to cry, and I said, Permission granted, and he settled his face between my breasts and moaned. When he was done, I noticed that his face wasn't wet.

That's because I cry dry tears.

Oh. Is that an actual term? Dry tears?

Well, I have a theory that men don't actually cry less than women, they just do it differently. Since we never saw our fathers cry, we are each forced to invent our own unique method.

My dad cried.

He did? Wet?

Yeah. All the time.

Is it possible that *his* father cried? And thus taught his son?

Well, maybe, but also my mom had a sixteen-year affair.

I went to the bathroom and washed my vagina in preparation. I paused in the hallway before returning to the bedroom; I could see him kneeling on my big square bed, staring fiercely at the lamp. He was bringing his penis to an erect position by choking it with both hands. It was easy to remember him sitting in his chair in his office, observing, nodding, producing a hard-won chuckle. I decided, right there in the darkness of the hallway, that I wanted this. If you'll be my man forever, I'll be your woman, Ed Borger. He suddenly stopped his furious hand movements and turned his head directly toward me in the shadows. As if he had heard me, as if responding to my vow. I waved. But he wasn't looking at me, he was looking behind me. I knew before I even turned around, it was Lyon.

Four excruciating interactions immediately followed this moment; the fifth was the drive to her parents' house. Lyon refused to sit beside me in the passenger seat.

Why should I?

Because it makes me feel like a chauffeur when you sit back there.

But you are a chauffeur.

Lyon.

What? Aren't you basically a babysitter chauffeur? Isn't that what my parents pay you for?

You know they don't pay me.

Well, that's your problem, not mine.

Lyon, we're a family.

No, actually, you are not related to us, you are just a person who used to help us the way Ed used to help us. It's really perfect that you two should fuck. All the hired help should fuck each other. I am in favor of it. We're all in favor of it.

Please don't tell Sarah and Tom.

Duh.

Duh you won't or duh you will?

Just duh.

But she didn't. She also didn't spend the night at my house again. She treated me like a friend of her parents, rushing past the three of us with her boyfriend, shouting, Bye, y'all, with a wave. This change was buried among all the other changes, the learning to drive, the perpetual sarcasm, the feminism. Tom and Sarah assured me that she ignored them, too, that we were all in the same boat, the one we came in on. But I knew. I blamed myself for all of this so-called individuation; it had sprung from a single moment. The guilt was crushing; it was the kind of thing I really should have talked to a therapist about. In moments I thought of calling Ed, as a professional. But would he be an objective outsider? He would not. The more I thought about this nonobjectivity, the more I wanted to call.

Dr. Borger.

Hi, Ed, it's Deb.

Deb, hi.

So, we haven't talked in a while.

What's on your mind?

Well, you never called me back after that day.

I didn't think it was appropriate to pursue a relationship after what happened.

Lyon doesn't even sleep at my house anymore, so it's not like she would even know.

Do you miss her?

Yeah, of course.

So this isn't really about me, is it?

Well, it is, in a way. You were involved.

Deb?

Yeah?

I hate to do this, but I need to call you back when I'm not in my office. Do you want me to call you back?

Do you want to?

If you want me to, I do.

But if I don't want you to, then you're totally fine with not calling?

I think it might be best if we let this go.

Inelegantly and without my consent, time passed. My relationship with Tom and Sarah became occasion-based: I was invited to Lyon's high school graduation, Tom's birthday, Thanksgiving, Christmas dinner. Lyon didn't come home from college for Christmas, but she sent the three of us UBCO sweatshirts from the University of British Columbia at Okanogan. She went faster and farther than I had imagined possible; who goes to college in Canada? Under financial duress, she came back for summer vacation, lived at home, and got a job at a lesbian-owned-and-operated organic produce market. I shopped there more than was necessary, but I didn't ask if she missed me, I didn't try to get back together, I kept the conversation light.

Excited to see you have the Saturn peaches in.

Don't thank me; they're not my Saturn peaches.

Well, technically, they are. Isn't this place worker-owned?

Yeah, but you have to work here for more than a summer and, like, eat the manager's pussy or something. Do you want a bag?

I joined PFLAG (Parents and Friends of Lesbians and Gays). I bought books by and for lesbians and their supportive, surprised parents. When she went back to school I imagined her sitting in a dorm with her arm around a young woman's waist, perhaps a young butch woman. I had read about the butch/femme dynamic and was sure that Lyon would be the femme. I wondered if Tom and Sarah knew about Lyon's preference; my guess was that they did not because they were still quite self-involved. They probably had fewer dalliances, but a bitterness had replaced the mania; the past now looked almost carefree. In December, Tom called to invite me to Christmas dinner.

Lyon will be there. She's coming home.

Oh, great.

And she has a new boyfriend. You're going to flip out when you meet him.

I quit PFLAG and moved through the next few days in weepy wonderment. I knew nothing about her. It was really over and I really was not her mother. I was really almost fifty. I really did not feel okay about any of this, and there was really nothing I could do about it. Somehow losing the lesbianism, the butch girlfriend, the need for tolerance, was worse than losing Lyon herself, years before. Or, more likely, I was still feeling the old loss, just in a new way.

I arrived late. Lyon wasn't even there; Tom and Sarah said she would show up by dessert. I talked to their other friends, some of whom I knew from our college days. I marveled at their nonchalant relationship to Lyon. One man thought she was still in high school. Just as we sat down for dinner, the doorbell rang. Someone in a puffy down jacket stumbled in, unwrapping his scarf. It was Ed Borger. He waved and said, Hi, everyone. And then he said, Lyon's coming, she's finishing a phone call.

These words were lost on me because I was consumed with Ed's shirt. It was a particular kind of modern dress shirt, a reproduction of a dress shirt that would have been popular in the sixties but had been modified to appeal to people who could not remember the sixties. Therein lay the problem, because Ed Borger *would* remember the sixties, he would remember being a teenager in the sixties, and he would avoid such a shirt because it would not seem retro to him, it would just remind him of a time before he had really gained social confidence. So someone else must have bought this shirt for him, a person who could not remember the sixties. My thoughts were interrupted by Lyon's entrance, her hand gently rubbing Ed's back as she said her hellos. Tom poured a glass of wine for Ed.

So, how's the family counseling business?

I can't complain, Tom.

We ate quietly, those of us who knew Ed and those of us who only knew there was a funny feeling in the room.

I guess that's true, you really *can't* complain, can you?

We ate our yam casserole and our scalloped potatoes and our baked ham.

What are you saying, Tom?

Ed placed his hand over Lyon's hand; we all looked from Ed to Tom. Tom looked at Lyon; we all did. She was staring intently at Sarah, who slowly looked up from her plate and at her daughter. And then, casually, Lyon slipped her hand out from beneath Ed's and passed me the potatoes, though I had not asked for the potatoes. I took the dish and she did not release the dish and we held the dish together for a moment, it hovered over her parents' dinner table. My eyes ventured slowly from the dish, to the front of her blouse, to her eyes. What did I fear I would find there? Meanness and gloating? Slyness? Shame? They were sparkling with the old love, the greatest love of my lifetime. And they were triumphant.

Acknowledgments

I'd like to thank each of these people for their part in helping me make this book: Fiona Maazel, Rick Moody, Nan Graham, Sarah Chalfant, and Mike Mills.

"The Shared Patio" was previously published in *Zoetrope*.

"The Man on the Stairs" was previously published in *Fence*.

"This Person" was previously published in *Bridge*.

"It Was Romance" was previously published in *Harvard Review*.

"Something That Needs Nothing" appeared in *Bridge* and *The New Yorker*.

"The Boy from Lam Kien" was originally published by Cloverfield Press.

"Making Love in 2003" appeared in *The Paris Review*.

"The Moves" appeared in *Tin House*.

"Birthmark" was previously published in *The Paris Review*.

About the Author

MIRANDA JULY is a filmmaker, writer, and performing artist. Her work has been presented at sites such as The Kitchen, the Guggenheim Museum, and two Whitney Biennials. She wrote, directed, and starred in her first feature-length film, *Me and You and Everyone We Know,* which received a special jury prize at the Sundance Film Festival and the Caméra d'Or at the Cannes Film Festival. Her short fiction has been published in *The Paris Review, Harper's, Zoetrope,* and *The New Yorker.* Raised in Berkeley, California, she currently lives in Los Angeles.

2/08/2 ℗

ABOUT THE AUTHOR

Widely known novelist—*The Volcano God, The Dark Shore, The Zoltans*—poet, short-story writer and literary critic, PHILIP FREUND is also the author of numerous plays and films. Over the past several years he has been on the faculties of Fordham University, Cornell University, Hunter College, the City College of New York, and the University of British Columbia, where has has lectured on a wide range of subjects, from creative writing in all its aspects to the history of films, art, music, and Oriental drama. He has published more than thirty-five books of fiction and nonfiction, the most recent being novellas collected in *The Beholder* and *The Devious Ways*.

ABOUT THE ILLUSTRATOR

A graduate of Pratt Institute and the Art Students League, MILTON CHARLES is the recipient of many national art and design awards and has been honored on several occasions with one-man shows. Mr. Charles is co-owner of Charles & Cuffari, Inc., a graphic arts studio designing for publishing, industrial, and commercial firms.

The text of this book was set by American Book–Stratford Press, Inc., in Linotype Baskerville, a recutting of the type face that was originally designed by John Baskerville (1706–75). The printing was done by Halliday Lithographic Corp. The binding was done by American–Stratford. The paper is #66 Antique offset by The S. D. Warren Co.